I0537620

The Kinky Side of Perfect

The Story Of A Good Girl's Erotic Introduction To The Enticing And Profitable Webcam World

By Star Sugarman & D.C. West

Win City Publishing
www.KinkyPerfect.com

Warning: This erotic story contains adult themes and explicit sexual situations including (but not limited to) exhibitionism, voyeurism, webcams, masturbation, group sex, adult toys, and passionate scenarios.

CONTENTS

DEDICATION i

ACKNOWLEDGMENTS iii

PROLOGUE v

CHAPTER 1 1

CHAPTER 2 11

CHAPTER 3 25

CHAPTER 4 31

CHAPTER 5 35

CHAPTER 6 49

CHAPTER 7 53

CHAPTER 8 65

CHAPTER 9 73

CHAPTER 10 81

EPILOGUE 87

DEDICATION

This book is dedicated to all who live their life's passion while in search of the mastery of perfection.

ACKNOWLEDGMENTS

First and foremost, I would like to acknowledge Almighty God from whom all Blessings flow. I would also like to thank my writing partner, D.C. West. To all of my Star Babies, my readers, my fans, thank you for your support, for all of your letters, and for sharing how deeply my stories of passion inspire you. May you continue to greet each day with Love and Curiosity. May each day greet you right back with a sweetness, like a warm blanket of hugs, smiles, kisses, and a touch of excitement for us all.

-Star Sugarman

As writers, we write because we must. As readers, you read because you choose. Thank you for choosing to read our stories and our words. To everyone who has been an inspiration of the past and of the present, I appreciate your contributions to my lore and my legends and for stimulating me to tap these keys and put these words to paper.

- Yours Truly, D.C. West

PROLOGUE

My Nana used to tell me, "Ships at a distance hold every woman's wish on board."

Of course she had never left the little town in Alabama where she was born. Her whole life, she kept diaries full of unfulfilled dreams and wishes. I grew up determined not to go out like that.

So, my favorite response to her was always, "Nana, 'Nothing comes from dreamers but dreams.'"

I didn't tell her that it was a verse from a Prince song because she would have called it 'Devil music' but the next line always resonated with me the most, 'sitting idle in a boat while everyone else is down the stream'. Those words were not a part of my values nor my vocabulary: dreams, sitting still, or being idle.

I look up at the expansive, luxurious cruise ship in the port before me now. I smile to myself, raise a metaphorical toast, and say, "This voyage is for you, Nana Redman."

I savor the salty, sweet smell of the Pacific Ocean as it smacks the San Diego shores. With the exception of a sweltering, half-day cruise in middle school, I have never been out on the ocean before. And I most certainly have never set foot on such a magnificent vessel as the one that I am about to board now.

The Kinky Side of Perfect

As I walk on the pier, my entourage includes my female butler, Theresa, and two porters, all three of whom were provided courtesy of the ship's Captain. At the gangplank, he greets me warmly, by name, and assures me that he had personally selected this team that would be on call for me 24/7 during our travels.

One porter walks in front of me while the other two bring up the rear, rolling two carts of my bags, which consists of nine matching, rich gold and brown Louis Vuitton pieces, including the classic steamer trunk. Oh, if they only knew what was in those bags.... The toys alone would titillate them. I had to pay good money to have my bags checked by a trusted comrade, thanks to my team's pre-planning. I laugh again and pinch myself one more time. I have been doing that a lot lately, but this day was extra special.

I continue up the long the gangplank, hearing the familiar whistles and catcalls, this time from the seamen working the lines of the ship. They gawk openly and a few boldly try to sneak a peek up my skirt as it flutters in the warm ocean breeze. I feel that chill and goose bumps appear across my body, but it isn't from being cold. It is from those waves of excitement, that very familiar thrill. Earlier this morning, I debated throwing on that red lace thong, but decided to go without it.

So, here I am, completely au naturale. I hadn't counted on the winds being this strong at the port. The afternoon breeze takes the skirt of my dress in every direction. Instead of continuing to make the futile effort to hold it down, I just walk proudly, naughtily letting let it blow in the wind. Go ahead fellas - enjoy my commando show for free while you can.

OMG, did I really just think that? Just a year ago these feelings and images...this sexual confidence... would never have even crossed my mind. Yet, at this instant, my body reacts with a

Pavlovian response, pulsing and throbbing, to all of the lustful stares being beamed in my direction.

Not too long ago, this whole center of attention stuff would have made me squeamish. After all, they were staring at me as if it were Thanksgiving, and I was the juicy, golden brown bird spread out on the table about to be served. But now, with everything I'd experienced over the past year, I handle it all in stride. A coy wave here, a flirty smile there, and a seductive wink or two for the most respectful admirers.

For example, the uber courteous, handsome, young porter helping me up the walkway got a wink and a smile. He holds my hand tightly, protectively, just a tad longer than necessary. I glance through my luxurious lashes, and look him up and down. He turns away trying to make an extra effort not to stare at my size 38DD tatas overflowing from the top of my sexy sundress.

I think to myself cynically, "Yeah, your sweet, exotic man-child charm doesn't fool me dude."

I finally learned, after 35 years, that even the nicest, sweetest guy can in fact be a big, closeted freak.

But who am I to talk? Just a year ago, I TOO was the nice, sweet, good girl. Look at me now, a stone-cold, unapologetic cyberfreak queen, having the time of my life, and making crazy money from it as well.

He continues to struggle to keep his eyes above my breast line. I smile reassuringly. He looks back comfortably and discretely caresses my hand. Ah, the power of subtext.

But enough of all this psycho-sexual Masters and Johnson's analysis. Enough work, pondering, and contemplation. This is a time for play and celebration. So many events have transpired to lead up to this amazing day. This next grand adventure.

I feel great and look even better than five years ago. I now own more fly clothes than ever in my life-- not just Gap or Old Navy like most of my adult life but, rather, top notch boutique brands. My red bottom Louboutin heels are on point, my long gel nails are glistening in the sun, and my fresh Remy hair extensions are down to my ass - top quality only, baby.

After months of living a double life, it is thrilling to now openly flaunt my new found sensuality and haute couture style without reserve. None of these people on this ship know me or my secrets. I can be whoever I want to be. I can do what I want without anyone in my business. I sigh with the relief of not having to keep secrets, like at home or deal with fake-ass, backstabbing people, like those at work.

We enter the ship and make our way straight past the lines of eager passengers checking in. I watch others signing up for port activities, assisted by a hierarchy of grinning, over-accommodating cruise staff.

A sun-burned, young brunette walks over and asked "Good afternoon ma'am would you like to sign up for sunset yoga lessons?" She flashes a look that says "Please help me get this commission...please." I knew the feeling, grin and bear it, the requirements of great service.

I smile back and reply, "Sure, sign me up. Suite #0003."

The woman looks at her tablet and responds, "Ms. Roxy Redman. The Emerald Suite. Very, very nice. Thank you Ms. Redman. Look forward to seeing you there!"

I nod but giggle to myself because I wonder if Aaron and I will even leave our rooms or the ship at all. Maybe, we will stay wrapped up in each other for the bulk of the journey.

The older, heavier porter, Jacques, interrupts my drifting thoughts by telling me to watch my step on the thick carpet. After all, I am wearing stilettos. He takes my arm and helps guide me as we round the corner. Even though he is my same height, his grip is strong and protective.

"Merci," I answered in his native language of French as noted by the red, white, and blue flag on his name tag.

We arrive at a private door with a golden handle. Jacques punches a code in the keypad. It opens to a small sitting room. There is a floor-to-ceiling mirror, a plush couch, and more roses, beautifully illuminated by gigantic windows.

We walk to an elevator door on the far side of the room and Jacques pushes the call button. The bell rings and we board. I have always enjoyed the feeling of a rising elevator, especially when exploring a new destination.

When the elevator opens, we step into another narrow corridor that has just one door with a sign reading "Emerald Royale Suite".

The porter swipes a key to unlock it. He smiles and speaks courteously "Welcome to your new home, Ms. Redman."

He dramatically flings the door open, revealing two beautifully styled, spacious stories. The entire décor is done in smooth cream ivory, tile, silver, and wood accented with radiant gold trim. It includes a first floor with two bedrooms, a kitchen, formal dining room, and living rooms connected with a spiral staircase and a private elevator which leads up to the master bedroom.

The Kinky Side of Perfect

My mind wanders again, this time to visions of lovemaking sessions on those stairs or in that elevator. Oh yes, this queenly palace will be my home for my week at sea. I saunter around the perimeter, taking my time to soak in the spacious living room. It is adorned with huge windows that are lined with billowing curtains, offering me, the lucky resident, and my guests, a most delicious view of the ocean on the starboard side. This also means that anyone outside could have a full view whenever I choose to walk around nude, which is my favorite way to be nowadays.

In the center of the room is a white baby grand piano with the top up. From habit and piano lessons from childhood, I walk over and gently play an arpeggio from middle C to high C. The sound reverberates lightly in the air filling the room with a sense of beauty, lightness and cheer. Just as delightful is the presentation of chocolates, caramel candies, red wine, luscious cheeses, and classic books spread out around the room.

"Where would you like your things Ma'am?" the fine porter asks.

I peer at his name tag, "Thank you, Isaiah… the living room is fine. Theresa, can you please organize my gowns and personal effects in the bathroom and bedroom? Don't mind the small bag, I'll unpack that myself."

Delegation and clear communication are two other new habits that have formed over the past year while I have been building and growing this venture. I found that stating the names of strangers upon meeting them helped me remember names and faces better. After juggling all of my own online and offline aliases, working with our freelance team, plus conducting more than a hundred live interviews, I learned how to keep my data better organized in my mind, in my ledgers, and in my cyberworlds.

It is amazing to think that just a year ago, I lived in my own head so often that I barely recognized the faces of my own co-workers or even the day of the week for that matter. Instead, I obsessed over other trite details, small, odd things like macromolecules, measuring proteins, DNA, or polysaccharides. I laugh thinking of those absent-minded, lab rat days.

I walk into the gorgeous dining area. It reminds me of a friend's San Francisco loft, narrow, sleek, wood paneling, and state of-the-art everything.

I grab a bottle of orange juice from a beverage cooler, mix in a splash of champagne, and raise a glass. My first celebratory mimosa. There is so much to celebrate.

I whisper a silent toast, "Here's to you Roxy Redmond aka Ms. Kinky Perfect."

I sip my drink and head towards a long couch beneath a window in the living room. I take a sit, kick off my shoes, and finally settle in, ready to relax.

I think to myself, "Here I am on a cruise ship, on the ocean, with my lover for a week while our business runs itself! Who would have ever thought?"

I know this voyage is going to be fantastic and rejuvenating… at least as long as I can avoid those damn Titanic thoughts when we are in the middle of the ocean. I'm just saying….

The porters expertly arrange my items and bag in a matter of minutes. As I reach for my bag to tip them, Theresa gestures for me to keep my hand in my purse.

"Ma'am, traditionally, tips are paid on the last day of the cruise. A little white envelope will be left in your room with names on them, one for each person."

I look into Theresa's blue eyes and appreciate the earnest honesty with which she is trying to protect me.

"Thank you for your consideration and honesty, Theresa. I am aware of cruising culture. This may be my first voyage but I always do my homework. I also like to show people that I value and reward their good service, loyalty, and discretion."

Among the many lessons I learned over this past year is that money does indeed talk. Or, as Aaron always says, "the presidents set the precedents." I love his savvy business mind...among other things. Ooh, the anticipation.

I tip the male porters each a crisp one hundred dollar bill, extending the green through my fresh long, red nails knowing that these two will now be good allies for the duration of the trip.

Jacques, the senior porter, replies graciously, "Miss Redman, thank you for your generosity and your kindness. Please let us know if there is anything we can do."

"Thank you," I say with a smile, "Theresa, I would like to speak with you privately for a moment."

The male porters courteously excuse themselves closing the palatial door behind them.

"Theresa, thank you for helping me with my personal items. During this week, I will also need your assistance on some of my work days. Please bring breakfast and let's be ready to start at 7am daily, except Thursday."

"Yes Ma'am."

"Additionally, I follow a strict regimen of vigorous exercise three times per week, yoga twice a week, daily massages and sessions in the steam room."

"Yes Ma'am, of course Miss Redman, I have this on the schedule as well. Mister Aaron Edwards has given me specific instructions for your care. I am here to provide the assistance you need," she says in her New England accent.

"Thank you, that's good to know, we appreciate your service. Also, please call me Roxanne."

Theresa nods affirmatively, "Yes Ma'am, Ms. Roxanne."

"Lastly, also regarding your... ah... discretion." I smile, thrilled by the thoughts. "You know, the things you may see...or hear during our stays. There are some who would pay you well to share secrets..."

Theresa interrupts me, "Most respectfully ma'am, I have maintained this position here for nearly 10 years. Funny thing is, I seem to have few recollections of memories of the past decade." She smiles for the first time.

I hand her two more crisp hundred dollar bills. She accepts them quite modestly.

"Thank you Miss Roxanne," she says. "Please let me know if there is anything else I can do to make your trip pleasant and memorable."

I nod as she heads towards the door and exits the room. I double-lock the door behind her.

I turn around, immediately overcome with serenity and gratitude. I am visually awestruck by the cinematic horizon visible through the panoramic windows all around me. I am audibly hypnotized by sounds of the ship's engine, gentle waves, seagulls, and the distant, happy chatter of active passengers. I feel euphoric and giddy. I sip my mimosa and steal a moment to soak in the splendor.

"Oh yeah, I can get used to this," I think as I run my fingers through my hair.

During the prior year and a half, I had watched as an abundance of opportunities and miracles presented themselves before me. Many were the results of my ideas, my plans and my efforts, but even more were simply the results of timing, grace, and sheer luck. Great genes and healthy curves helped too. Lol.

I think of my former ways, my life before cams and after cams. Denise calls this BC and AD ("before cams" and "after doin' it'") but the religious part of me doesn't go for that. All I know is that my former routines have been transmuted from mundane, unassuming, and predictable into grand, adventurous, passionate and mind-blowingly profitable, albeit a bit risky and risque at times. I...we... or rather our team, has far surpassed all the business goals we set and more. It has taken tremendous time and hustle but the payoff, the dividends, are in hand, and even bigger payouts are on the horizon.

I feel waves of gratitude and whisper aloud, "Thank you, God!"

I tuck my feet under me on the couch, and turn toward the sun so that it can caress my cheeks and warm my entire body. I lounge and get comfy in my dream suite.

While the financial success continues to be a tremendous turn on, it now pales in comparison to the lightning flashes of excitement that strike every time I think of the fact of my soon to be real life lover and my business partner, Aaron Edwards, is arriving. Somewhere on his journey, right now, he is too is pondering and planning our rendezvous.

Finally, after 16 super prosperous months of long distance business, and now a budding romance, my cyber-muse and I will meet, in person, for the first time. After all of the phone sex, cybersex, and sexting, I can finally open my lips and legs for him and feel him in person. I craved a thousand kisses and a hundred orgasms, every day!

Denise was usually super cynical about the prospects of cyberdating. But, it is because of her that Aaron and I met and hooked up in the first place. Still, she told me before I left home, "Girl, we have made a lot of money working with Aaron, and he is hot and definitely packing. But don't get your hopes up too high cause 97.98 percent of the time real chemistry doesn't match the online chemistry. Just look at the show Catfish. That shit is real. Don't you go fucking up this good business thing we got here even when y'all think you are falling in loooove. For real. You hear me?"

She had booked Aaron's room all the way on the port side, at the complete opposite end of the ship, just in case anything was off or if we needed personal space during our voyage.

Aaron, forever practical, had no problems with Denise's rationale.

"You know me, baby," he had said. "I'm ordinarily all about business over pleasure and the money before honey! But since you got my head and heart all twisted around, I may not be thinking straight. So, I'm going to trust Denise's call on that."

And so we agreed that if, on the contrary, we do click as we hoped, then my innocent, girly-girl styled room would become known as The Sweet Suite while his masculine, geek-inspired, minimalistically styled room would be labeled The Freak Suite. It was our own little private, horny joke.

Aaron had started as my webmaster and business partner but has grown to be so much more. Our first goal was to build a successful business together, but we also learned that we enjoyed collaborating in many other ways.

The Kinky Side of Perfect

At the beginning, our personalities could not have been more different. I was reserved, conservative, and aloof. He was spontaneous, expressive, and charming. I lived in SoCal, he lived up North in the Bay. He was a self-made entrepreneur who grew up in the foster care system with no family. I always had the tremendous support of my loving but nosey family. I had to work hard to keep them out of my business, personal and otherwise.

Despite these contrasts, through months of online and phone chats, Aaron and I found that we shared many similar values regarding business, art, and life. Before long, we were yearning for the day that we would choose a neutral location and finally meet face-to-face, body-to-body, and mind-to-mind. We could have connected months ago, the money and time were there. But early on, we set a financial goal. We said that within one month of achieving our goal, we would meet and finally consummate our union. That day is today.

After the sterile, passionless years with Victor, I love the butterflies I feel in my stomach and the fire in my veins for Aaron. Just the thought of him warms me from head to toe. I feel like a teen girl opening her first cards and candy on Valentine's Day.

Of course, the romantic side of me hopes for the best but the pragmatic side of me prepares to handle the worst. Either way, I am doing my best to keep calm and carry on.

Because the fact is that no matter whether or not we have real sparks, there is no denying that at this very moment, our adult cam site, KinkyPerfect.com, is earning $15,000 - $30,000 per day, even while I sit here sipping this mimosa and spacing out.

We have put in an immense amount of diligent work and effort to build this brand. Now, finally, it is exceeding our expectations. We just have to keep it steady and move forward on our designated course, just like this ship.

All of a sudden, the aphrodisiac of success, the pleasantries of the cruise, and sweeping thoughts of Aaron, combine and hit me with a super-hot wave of horniness. We still have another four hours until our determined meeting time as he is not expected to arrive until later. I may as well break in the new place and get comfortable.

I adjust my head and shift the silk pillow under my neck. I lift my red dress and gently slide it up my thigh, enjoying the feeling of the soft fabric on my skin. A gust of sea air brushes my body with a warm caress. Then, the breeze wraps its way around my leg, kissing me squarely between my thighs. I could hear Aaron saying, "Hmm, now would be a good time to relax sweetheart and savor the moment, enjoy that."

I think about his voice, our enterprises, and creative cybersex sessions. Without a second delay, my hand is between my legs. I open my thick thighs and spread my legs wide, like bands of milk chocolate draping across the ivory colored couch.

Yes, I enjoy that the windows were open and feel I like a straight nudist. An exhibitionist becoming one with nature.

I unbutton the top of my dress, and began to trace my hands over the bra covering my full, round, mocha breasts-- now known as "the tits that started it all." I laugh at Aaron's profound and frank way with words.

He was right. Had I not so nervously flashed these lovely chocolate nipples on cam that evening, none of the other events would have ever occurred. None of the self-discovery, pleasure, notoriety, or, and certainly, none of the money.

The Kinky Side of Perfect

Right now though, my nipples are getting hard and straining through the laciness of my bra. With a gentle scoop of my hands, I twist one breast free and then liberate the other. I hear a foghorn and I feel a new motion as the ship begins to pull away from the port.

I smile to myself and say, "Bon Voyage."

I lick my finger tip and put it back down to my nipple, and begin to gently twirl it. The wetness and the breeze give me little goosebumps I moan feeling my nipples harden fully and stand firm at attention, looking like two sweet tootsie rolls tips in the middle of luscious, giant cupcakes, ready to be licked and nibbled.

I slide my other hand back under my skirt and touch myself. I am so wet. I rub some of the lubrication on my swollen clit. I tease the hood and make slow circles around it.

I hadn't planned to cum before seeing Aaron but the more I think of the reality of our circumstances, the more aroused I become. I keep a thumb on my clit and slip my finger inside of myself. I see images and thoughts of him, this suite, the money, our business, our fans, the journey, all we have accomplished, and the thrill of being with him for the first time.

We will be making love shortly. I will finally feel him inside me and taste him with my mouth.

I throw my head back and squirm on the couch, imagining the hardness of his shaft. I slide two fingers of my free hand to my mouth and suck the tips of them hard. I wish it was the head of his dick. I slide the fingers deeper in my mouth, wanting to feel him down my throat.

I fuck my mouth with my fingers and rub my pussy faster and harder. I groan and cum intensely, squirting all over my pretty couch, moaning loudly for all the world to hear. Fortunately, my screams of passion are covered by the sounds of the fog horn, the ship's motors, and the cheering crowd.

I pant in my post orgasmic Zen, and lay there in reverie with my legs still open. The sun rays illuminate my mostly naked body and shimmer throughout the luxurious suite. At that moment, everything is, in fact, quite perfect. I slide over away from the damp spot, put a pillow between my thighs, and think of Aaron's imminent arrival. Titillated and serene, I doze off into a most comfortable, relaxed sleep.

CHAPTER 1

18 Months Earlier --

"Knock, knock!", Bryce's nasal voice chimed over the partition beside my office desk before I even logged onto my computer.

I cringed and put on my game face, team-player smile. "Good Morning, Bryce," I said through gritted teeth. I dialed up my civility, "How can I help you?"

"Beautiful, I am sure that there are many ways you could help me or we could help each other." He smiled in a most politically inappropriate manner.

Bryce was an annoying, 48 Laws-of-Power-quoting, pretentious, bow-tie wearing, twit. Bryce was pretty popular, especially with the ladies in the office. And even more so with the ones who were privy to the information that his father, Nicholas Clarke, was a respected venture capitalist on the board of this multi-billion dollar company.

Even when he sat in on my interview before I had been hired three years ago, Bryce had tried to upstage or minimize everything I did. I, on the other hand, was taught early to first and foremost compete with yourself and not to make it a goal to out-do everyone else.

This fool, however, had a well-documented habit of mimicking and even cloning my words, my ideas, and truly believing that he had come up with them, like some sort of pathological liar. He had eavesdropped on my calls, looked over my shoulder, listened outside a door, and asked others for information about me. Oh, but he'd never ask me directly about anything significant. Then, next thing I knew, he was presenting my ideas as his own at meetings.

The thing is, he knew that there would be one spot opening for a partner in the company, and he wanted it. He also knew that I was eligible for the position as well.

All through college, I had been courted by a myriad of impressive companies. I raked up great internships and international study opportunities. After working at one successful company after another, navigating thru the ranks, I finally secured a coveted position at O'Neal Labs, one of the top laboratories in the country.

It was a nanotech, research and engineering firm owned by one of my idols, Annette O'Neal. Annette, too, had graduated at the top of her class, but at MIT. She had a bunch of patents, and now ran her own, highly profitable, venture capital funded lab. I wanted to be like her. Next to me, she had the highest work ethic of anyone in the field. She worked and lived at that lab almost 24/7.

Although his Dad made him start as an intern, Bryce still took full advantage of his spoiled, princely, nepotistic position. All that said though, the man was a genius. He was a great problem-solver except for his own problem of blind ambition and that grand grandiose sense of self.

His father, Nicholas, on the other hand, was a true dynamo of an entrepreneur. A vibrant, handsome gentleman with salt and pepper hair from the Southwest, his 73 patents alone were worth hundreds of millions of dollars. He was a legend in the industry, but he was still one of the most modest, humble, billionaires I'd ever met (which was many by that time). He drove a hybrid SUV and dressed in jeans. I had met Nicholas on many occasions. Fortunately, he and I got along fine, really well actually, and this was primarily due to the fact that he was nothing like his son.

Nicholas actually had some similar qualities to my boyfriend Victor. Upstanding and driven, Victor was what you would consider all-American. Tall. Handsome. What Candace would probably think was most important was that he had money. Lots of it.

Victor was from a good family. Plus, he was well respected and well-liked. He had a great smile that would make you blush if you looked at him for any length of time. His skin was a deep mocha and he had a face that looked like it was chiseled by the hand of God directly.

He always wore his hair in a crew cut and got it shaped up weekly. He had played football in high school, now ran his own shipping store, and did everything by the book. And I do mean everything. I will tell you about our sex life in a minute, but first, let me tell you how we met.

Victor and I met through Dad about a year ago. They had met while Dad was negotiating one of his delivery contracts for Victor's location. So, of course, my parents adored him. They kept asking me, no pressure of course, when was the wedding, when could they start picking out bassinets, and when will we start thinking about our future?

I told them each time to have patience, that things would happen at their own pace. I loved Victor even though our time together was sometimes a little beige. By beige, I mean bland. But everything else about my relationship with him was as close to perfect as possible. Plus, I had to admit, he and I would make some absolutely adorable kids.

Unfortunately, while Victor had attributes much like Nicholas, Bryce did not. In fact, it was all too clear that Bryce inherited his lack of social graces from his mother, Clarissa. She reminded me of a brassy, mid-60s, real housewife version of Anna Nicole. But unlike Anna Nicole, she was crass to the core. Although she was still married to Nicholas, she had made more than a few overt comments and sexual advances towards me during my months working with the company.

The first time it happened, I was in an elevator returning from lunch. She walked in from the cafeteria floor carrying a company tote bag and a bowl of fruit. She smiled, was friendly, and made banter for a floor until the other two passengers exited.

When the door closed, and we were left alone, she said "Oh what I'd do to be sucking on your beautiful melons, instead of this cantaloupe Roxanne. Let me know when."

She winked at me, exited the elevator, and left me stunned as the door closed. Hmmm, perhaps this was the way some of my co-workers were getting ahead. Not me. Forget that!

Then, last winter, she cornered me by the bar at the office holiday party when Victor went to get our drinks. Clarissa was clearly feeling quite uninhibited from the champagne and an abundance of sexual energy generated from her low cut, hip-grabbing dress. While playing it absolutely cool, she let another couple push her close to me, with my back against the bar, her leg between my thighs discretely covered by the bar stools and masses of other people around them. She grinded to the DJ's rhythm, pressing on my leg and pushing her knee against my pelvis-- telling me that she would love to show me what it was like to be with a real woman.

I looked around shocked—didn't anyone see this heifer dry humping me? But everyone else in sight and earshot was absorbed in their own dance, humping, and grinding—buzzed and buzzing. I giggled uncomfortably, a reflex. Fortunately, Victor arrived with our drinks and helped me maneuver from her drunk grasp. Instead of making a scene, we quickly exited the party, skipped the line by telling the valet it was an emergency, and rolled out. Although things were dull with Victor sometimes, I appreciated him at that moment as he swept in as my hero.

Anyway, after having a mother like Clarissa, no wonder Bryce was the way he was I realized, as I stared at him standing at my desk.

"Annette and I were talking," Bryce continued. "I have a new process theory that she wants to try. She told me to set up a research team with anyone I wanted to be on my team. And, of course, I picked you as my first choice."

I took a beat. "Bryce, that's very kind of you but I have my projects and research to work on," I told him.

His strategy was quite clear. Keep your friends close and your enemies closer.

But, I didn't really consider him an enemy. It was more like a "watch ya back with a shady MF like that" type of situation, as my Daddy would say.

Bryce persisted, "I won't take no for an answer. As I come up in the ranks and gain all the glory that comes with it, I want you to be right there behind me," he said.

"Does he hear himself?" I wondered to myself. He didn't say "with", "next to" or "beside". He said "right there behind me" and on the deepest level, that is exactly what he meant.

"Bryce, thank you for thinking of me," I answered with a sugary sweetness. "But between my work here and spending time with my family and Victor, I just wouldn't have time." I smiled my best office politics smile, "You'll just have to go for the glory without me."

"Hmmm…ok," he said. "But I will be keeping an eye on you…in case any other opportunities come up on my team."

"As loved as you are here, I'm sure you will have no trouble finding someone else," I replied, puffing up his ego, while still smiling the office smile.

Dramatically, and in my face, Bryce made the "I've got my eye on you" gesture with his two fingers. Then he painted on his fake smile with those ultra-bright, veneered teeth gleaming against his olive skin and walked away.

He stared directly at me as he walked away, keeping his eyes locked on me. Where was my garlic and holy water when I needed it? I was so glad when he finally left my desk and took that nasty-smelling cologne with him. Somebody should have told him that just because it was expensive doesn't mean that it was supposed to be bathed in like a second shower.

My relief was short because the next thing I overheard was Bryce's voice quietly emanating from Annette's office saying that I wouldn't be joining his team after all even though he begged me and that he was starting to doubt my loyalty to the company. Oh, no he didn't!

I was unable to hear what, if anything, was Annette's response as Patricia, Annette's executive assistant, walked over and closed the door to give them some privacy. Of course, she looked over and caught me eavesdropping before I could look away. Dang! This office drama was too much.

Whatever. Fortunately, today was Tuesday and I was going over to Victor's tonight which would be a great way to relax. I always stayed at Victor's on Tuesdays and Fridays like clockwork, which meant I always had pseudo-sex twice a week, except on my period. Although, our relationship was a little bland, it was comfortable and familiar. TGIF.

Victor had a loft downtown with wooden beam ceilings, a polished chrome bachelor's kitchen, and a fully stocked bar. It was in the penthouse on the 18th floor so it also had a pretty cool view of other historic buildings in the city.

Now, back to our sex life. With all that natural chemistry, our love life should have progressed like something out of a steamy romance novel with "the heaving bosom" and "his manhood riseth", but instead it was the same super boring routine, every time. First, we would lay in the bed side-by-side, naked. Then, he would kiss me, quick and mechanically. That was his version of foreplay, bless him. Fortunately, it got my panties wet enough just looking at him across the bed. He was just that beautiful.

Then, he would come over slowly and go down on me. A quick lick, lick, lick for about one minute, and I do mean one. I should have been grateful that he went down on me at all because I know some women will never experience that in their entire lifetimes. Even so, I liked it ok, but it wasn't my personal favorite.

After that, he slid his body up mine where I was laying in missionary position. He rolled the condom on, rubbed the head of his beautiful dick between the lips down there, found the hole, and slid it in. We both moaned at that point because you and I both know that felt good.

The Kinky Side of Perfect

But then, he did this exact choreography, those three thrusts. Thrust, thrust, thrust. Then he would come, just like every time.

Right after that, he cleaned up, put that little black satin sleeping mask on, kissed me adoringly, and fell right to sleep. Snoring. Loudly. It could be a 3-alarm fire, earthquake, or a zombie apocalypse, and that man would stay asleep and would not wake up until the next day. But the most annoying thing was, at 5:31am, like clockwork, he woke up, took that little mask off, and said, "Good Morning!"

Years ago, when I read the J. California Cooper book, "In Search of Satisfaction", I never realized I would be living with that as the full reality of my sex life.... Shouldn't there have been more? I knew he cared about me though, and that's what really mattered. Right?

Lick, lick, lick. Thrust, thrust, thrust. Snoring. Good morning. Wash, rinse, and repeat. I was so deeply grateful for that state-of-the-art shower head he had at his place. Whenever I showered after our routine, that shower head made me cum the deepest I had ever cum in my life. I had to struggle to be quiet in there, it felt so good. Even when I made myself cum at home in bed, it felt good, but not this good. This was explosive. Yeah, it was my own scandalous, little secret.

As my thoughts drew me out of the shower, I emerged in the now as I continued getting my ear hustle on to hear the rest of Bryce's conversation with Annette. His words driven by ruthless ambition. I was interrupted by the sound of my phone ringing loudly. It was a call from my best friend, Denise. I loved her dearly but even dealing with her drama took a certain type of patience.

I had forgotten to turn my ringer off. So, I got dirty looks from a couple of the other researchers when my ringtone echoed through the lab. I clicked the "off" button and sighed deeply.

It was going to be a long day.

CHAPTER 2

I had never been one to wear my sexuality on my sleeve. I could never relate to those women whose sex appeal was their primary identity or those who wore and flaunted their assets like a garment they take on and off.

True, like most other babies of the 80's, I grew up seeing sex all around me – bouncing, bodacious breasts and big asses spread all over the media, tv programs, and expensive ads.

I could never respect those music video vixens or the women in magazine ads and commercials whose sole purpose was to entice their viewers, encouraging the suckers who were willing to buy something-- anything.

Yes, like my sister and some of my girlfriends, I could have had sugar daddies footing my bills since before I was of legal age. How hard is that in this day and age?

In high school, I had been hit on by fiendish old men, some young ones too, and more than a few women on a nearly daily basis, when all I was doing was simply riding the bus between school and home.

Instead, from a very young age, I worked hard to maintain my reputation as a good girl. I kept my breasts completely covered up, dressed down to hide my curves, refused to draw attention to my full lips, and buried my almond eyes behind the least attractive, thick lenses I could find – anything I could do to keep them more focused on my mind than my behind.

I had been more determined to outthink my way to the top than to out fuck my way to the top. Just as some women relished in being branded "the slut", I had cherished my "good girl" status and reputation that included perfect attendance, straight A's and Honor programs. I even had a patent in my own name before I was 18.

That was a commitment I had made to myself at a very young age. To start each day with new joy, no matter what challenges I had faced the days before. I had developed this particular resolve after watching my big sister's struggles and torment out in the streets, jail, and rehab over the years. I saw, firsthand, the pain and misery it caused her and our parents.

As a creature of habit and discipline, I woke up at the exact same time every day. No alarm required. I'd lay in the same full size bed that I'd had slept in since high school, except for the four years I was away at grad school. I'd take a moment to breathe, while I prepared my mind to attack my day with zeal and enthusiasm.

As soon as my toes touched the ground, I would grab the jug next to my bed and drink a full 32 ounces of spring water, before anything else. My Nana said that clean water, good food, hard work, great sex and sound sleep were the keys to health. She had lived to be 101 years old, so I tended to value her opinion when it came to longevity.

I maintained Nana's recommended regimen on all points, with the exception of the great sex part. While Victor and I had sex twice a week, it was far from great. It felt more like the mandatory penetration act for my boyfriend so he could sleep while I took care of myself. I remained optimistic though that things would get better.

My daily life ran by nice, simple systems and routines. For instance, I always brushed my teeth, flossed meticulously, and rinsed thoroughly for five minutes each. I always picked out a week's worth of clothing every Sunday afternoon and made sure the outfit for any specific day was set out the night before.

After a quick green smoothie and a stretch, I stepped outside for my daily jog and catch up on the latest news and gossip on my phone, while playing dance music in the background. I would keep it moving for 37 minutes with exactly 3 loops with 3 sets of calisthenics in between. I loved the fresh air, and being up and active before most of the world.

Plus, if I didn't get my workout in at the beginning of the day, I felt obsessively distracted the rest of the day. When I had something on my calendar, I was not satisfied until I got it done. I was the same way with everything that I set my mind to. I always ran with the heart of a champion toward any finish line I had set for myself.

Back at home, after finishing my run, I would shower, put on the cute outfit that I had laid out, and brush my hair, making sure every strand was in place.

I would reach for my favorite perfume with a baby powder scent and spritz it on the same places every day. One wrist, the next wrist, then, I opened my legs and spritzed once. Now I was ready.

Looking over my outfit in the mirror, I made sure it was buttoned properly and covered my buxom cleavage. My skirt fit loosely, camouflaging my curvy hips and ass.

I would check the time on my phone, unplug it and slip it in my purse. Next, I would grab my keys and head downstairs to leave. Since it was usually barely seven o'clock on a Sunday morning, I was the first and only one up in our house.

The Kinky Side of Perfect

My Dad has had his own trucking company for nearly 20 years, so he always set his own hours. My Mom was almost always away on military assignments and stayed busy, even when she was home. My little brother, Everett, was also in the military and was stationed overseas.

My big sister, Candace, on the other hand, always moved to her own beat and rhythm. This was especially true since her most recent return from rehab. She also seemed to sleep a lot. Chances are she would probably just be waking up when I returned home from the lab this evening.

At least she wasn't out on the streets though, using meth, Lean, Molly, K2, turning tricks, or laid up under some pimp somewhere, like she used to be. Always the rebel, by the time she was a sophomore, she had tried nearly every kind of drug out there from over-the-counter stuff to heavy illegal narcotics. The church therapist had said she was trying to fill a void that could never be filled.

Once, when I was 14 and she had just turned 18, Candace ran away from home. My family spent weeks trying to find her and we eventually got word that she was staying with a guy named Flip who was a 32 year old narcotics dealer. He also moonlighted as a pimp for some of his top clients.

The curves in our family are legendary and hereditary. Like Mom, Candace had plenty of them by 18. Boom. Pow! But, unlike me, she loved to show them off, especially for older men. And Flip, like any good pimp, saw an opportunity and seized it. He lavished her with gifts and attention. He promised her the best of everything - designer clothes, Italian bags, and all the illicit, debilitating substances she could consume.

Flip kept his promise and for the first couple of weeks, she was a real-life princess. She was waited on hand and foot by his other girls. Like a treasured prize, she was kept away from the grimy men who regularly paid top dollar for fresh young coochie. Instead, he put her through training and taught her many new tricks of the trade. She was happy to learn because deep down, she was just happy to finally have somebody take a real interest in her.

She was a straight A student in that field and became skilled in the arts of what Flip called "Sloppy Seduction." With the help of his other girls, she learned how to lick circles when giving head, how to squeeze in a certain way to make clients cum and even how to twerk when doing it doggie style to create that extra friction.

When it was time, he took her to the house of a glamorous older whore, a busty Costa Rican woman in her 50s, Sofia, who had struck it rich when one of her long time tricks died and left her everything. She hated most men with a passion and craved the innocence of young women. But as Flip's sugar momma, she waited eagerly for his weekly visits with his newest, freshest girls.

She was the one who taught Candace how to spread the female client's pussy lips open, how to titillate their clits, how to tease them close to orgasm and make them wait with suspense, and how to massage the g-spot with fingers to make them cum repeatedly. When Flip brought Candace for her first visit, the three of them laid in her mansion, got smoked out, and fucked for days.

Then one evening, their fairy tale took a turn in another direction.

That day, after a particularly successful deal, Flip had turned to one of his clients and said with a handshake, "Great doing business once more. I got a little gift for you. Why don't you enjoy this fast, fine, young ass for a few hours."

15

He essentially began offering my sister up to the wolves. From that point on, despite her initial objections, he charged premium for her and began to pimp her out on the regular.

Candace started losing herself gradually as she became more and more strung out. If he had a new product, she had to try it, smoke it, snort it, inject it and pop pills whenever it was convenient. Ever the businessman, he gave her a constant supply, and, in turn, kept her indebted to him.

You better believe that after we found out where she was, she wasn't there long. I remember it all too clearly. My parents mobilized their military, cop, and trucker friends. They rolled up to the pimp's pad with a show of civic force.

Though I was only 14 and my little brother, Everett, was 11 at that time, my Mom insisted that we ride with her.

My Dad said, "I want you all to see this. You need to see the other side of the world, the grimy, dark side…where boys and girls are manipulated, brainwashed, drugged up, and sold from one person to the next, like furniture or cattle or slaves. It steals pieces of their lives and their spirits. They don't even know it till they wake up, years later--- bodies battered, aged, worn, and sickly. We are doing this to save your sister. We are doing this to save your future Roxanne, and you too, Everett."

By this time in her life, Mom had been on many tours overseas and, as a result, had handled some of the world's most dangerous fugitives. She wasn't afraid to fight for her beliefs. She and my Dad instilled that in us, too. My dad called some of his trucker friends and we all headed over, driven like on a holy mission.

"Oh yeah," I thought, "we were rolling in deep."

By the time we pulled up to Flip's house, it was 10pm. He lived in a one story 900 square foot house with flaking paint and a hole at the bottom left corner of the door from disrepair. This was his idea of laying low and staying under the radar. There were bars on both the windows and the doors, and the yard was a mess. Liquor bottles and beer cans littered the front grass, or what was left of it, and both the roof and the porch were falling apart from wood rot. Just nasty!

As much money as he had, you would think he would fix up the place or live somewhere else. But, I guess he was trying not to attract attention to himself by balling publicly. As we parked, I could see he had three cars tucked discreetly in the back - one average maroon four door sedan, probably for basic runs, and two new big black SUVs. Both trucks were gleaming, all waxed up with tinted windows and big chrome rims that shone so brightly that I could see them glittering from the moonlight's reflection in the dark even from as far away as we were parked.

"Stay here! And keep the doors locked," my Mom said as she climbed out of the car.

I crouched in the passenger seat and watched as my Mom stormed up to the house and banged on the door. Dad and his crew got out of their trucks and watched as well.

"Candace! Candace! Get your ass out here!" Mom yelled authoritatively.

The front door opened but the iron screen door did not.

"Ma'am, good evening. My mama taught me to be respectful to all ladies but Candace doesn't want to come with you," Flip said pimp talking smoothly in perfect English with a slight Southern tone through those gold and diamond teeth in the front of his mouth.

"You're welcome to visit her here though any time you like. Any kin to her is like kin to me. Besides, I am quite sure the fellas would like that," he said as he took his time looking over Mom's fit physique.

He saw a price tag on everything. Sleazy with a capital "S".

His friends were snickering in the background. Through the front window, I could see three or four of his boys in the living room playing some kind of commando video game. One put a big brown liquor bottle to his face and took a drink.

"Young man, it doesn't matter what the fuck you say. My daughter is coming with me. Now get out of my way," Mom said strongly.

"Oooh, Flip!" his boys said. "She told your ass," one of them said in a gravelly voice that sounded worn, a sound that could only come from years of sucking on a glass pipe (as I was to later learn).

"Man, Shut the hell up!" he yelled over his shoulder before he looked back at my Mom and smiled smugly.

He wore his inflated ego like it was a suit of impenetrable kevlar.

"Son, I am going to say it one more time. Then, I am coming in to get my child," she said while placing her hand on her weapon.

Flip peered through the screen, his eyes half-mast while he enjoyed the rest of his high.

"Bitch, how you gonna do that?" he asked, making a big mistake in calling my mother out of her name.

My Dad and his homies stepped out of their trucks, some of them brandishing their pieces.

The dude we call Big Unc J, rested a foot on his truck tire and said to Flip from the curb, "What we have here is a right-to-carry situation. Don't make things complicated, boy."

Without another word or any warning, my mother removed her sidearm and fired one shot at the lock on the screen.

Flip jumped back and said, "Oh shit!" Hi eyes no were longer squinted but round as saucers. His friends, with all their trash talking, scattered like roaches, dropping whatever was in their hands – game remotes, pipes, needles, drinks - and jumped behind the torn couch, run down chair, or whatever tattered piece of furniture they could find to hide behind.

Candace ran from somewhere in the back of the house and screamed, "Stop it!" while trying to stand upright.

She was obviously high. She teetered in some little slingback white high heels and a short orange halter dress trying to get her point across and cover her ass at the same time because it surely was hanging out.

Mom kicked the screen door and because the lock was gone, it bounced back open, swinging out over the porch.

With a syrupy reverence for fire power, Flip said, "Yo, mama. You got it. You got it...."

Flip had made another mistake in answering the door in just his drawers and a wife-beater with no weapon. He thought he was coming just to shoo some old lady off his porch.

She aimed her gun at his face. His hands flew up. His high was definitely ruined now. He could see in her eyes that she was

19

not afraid. Clearly, he had underestimated who he was dealing with.

"Candace Redman! Get out here. Now!" she yelled.

"Mom, I'm not leaving," Candace yelled back, with a nastiness I did not recognize.

That was obviously the drugs talking because she had never been this disrespectful before. Who knows what she had taken?

"Don't you back talk me. You get your ass outside. Right now!" Mom yelled, her voice a little louder.

"I ain't going nowhere with you, Mama!" Candace yelled. "Flip cares a hell of a lot more for me than you do. He is always here for me. You and Dad are always gone. You don't give a shit about me. You don't love me. You didn't even want me! You just want me to raise your other kids like a fuckin' 24/7 babysitter. I've had enough. I want out!" Candace screeched, still wobbling.

"Girl, shut the hell up. You don't know what you are talking about," Mom said.

She always did cuss like a sailor so she could dish it right back to Candace but she directed it to Flip instead.

"What the fuck did you give her you fucking pervert? She is barely 18!" Mom said. "You step back or I swear to God I will shoot those fucking cornrows off your head into the next room, call the cops myself, and tell them where to find your perverted ass body, you carbon copy, C-List, Don Juan wanna be. All these men are here not to protect me but to keep me from killing your trifling ass right here where you stand. And don't think you can come to our house either because I will have my Black Ops associates watching your ass. When I got through with you, I could get you gone so thoroughly the only thing left will be them gold teeth for your homies to pawn. Now move your got-damn muthafuckin' ass the fuck outta my way!"

Mom kept the barrel aimed squarely at his face as she reached in the doorway and pulled Candace by the arm.

Candace stumbled out of the house, unsuccessfully trying to struggle away.

"Mom! Stop it! Mama!" Candace screamed.

Our mother pretty much dragged her down the stairs to the car and put her in the back seat. Candace was so high.

When I turned around to look at her, even in the dark car, I could see her pupils were fully dilated. She looked like a hollow fiend of herself.

"Whatchu lookin' at!" she snapped at me.

Then, she slumped over in the backseat and started to cry. Everett was already crying. Tears just rolled down his little face. He was terrified at the snarling monster his big sister had become.

I looked back toward the house and saw that Flip was in the yard yelling all kinds of "Bitches", "Whores" and "MFs" at our cars as we sped off.

Even at 14, I could see that he was just trying to save face after being embarrassed in front of his boys. Plus, now he would have to find another gullible somebody to make that side money, with my sister was gone. It probably wouldn't take him long.

"Fuck!" I heard him yell angrily into the night but he knew better than to come after us.

I was glad because Mom surely would have shot him more than once. I looked over at her and noticed she hadn't put her gun back in the holster but had laid it flat on the seat until we were far away from his place, just in case. This woman truly had great combat strategy. Dad and his crew rolled with us taking up the rear, just in case, as an extra precaution.

We took Candace straight to Reaching Pines Rehabilitation Center and checked her in. She was screaming and crying the whole time while clawing at the staff and babbling something about letting her at least go back to get her designer clothes. Little did I know, this would foreshadow the next 20 years where she would be in and out of rehabs repeatedly.

Back then, I wondered if this cycle of treatment facilities was going to continue for the rest of her life. Eventually, her teeth and her looks were gone. My concerns were proven because by the time I was in grad school, she had become completely smoked out.

From that day at age 14 on, I did everything in my power to make sure that that would never be me.

I focused on my schoolwork and made great grades. I never made waves and was popular with both the teachers and students. My junior year of high school, I became class vice-president. If I ever needed motivation, I would think back to that night. No way I was going down like that. EVER!

In light of everything that had happened, Dad left his trucking job and opened his own freight and shipping company so he could stay close to home. He told me and my little brother, Everett, that he was always going to be there in arms' reach for us all of our lives. And from then on, he was....

That's also when our parents began our martial arts training. My mother was determined to not lose any more children to the temptations of the streets. Or, as she would say, "You MUST be able to survive whatever comes your way, whether we are with you or not."

Although Dad seemed to have accepted the fact that he couldn't control his wife's or son's fate in the face of militants and hostiles, he relished in the fact that now he could go to sleep knowing his girls are safe. He never seemed to be able to let go of the idea of not being able to always protect and rescue his daughters.

Still reminiscing, I got ready to head into work. I unlocked the car with the remote, climbed in, drove to the coffee spot drive thru and ordered my usual, a grande house with 4 creams and 6 sugars. I scanned my phone coupon to get the discount and to rack up the points on my loyalty card. Ah yes, that amazing raw sugar, that creme, caffeine combination, delish. Ok, now, I was ready to go to work.

My career was on both a schedule and a track that I had charted long ago, back in elementary school. The plan was to finish high school, go to college, work a couple of years, go to grad school, work a few more years, save some money, get married in my late 30s, have children, and retire while living off of my invention royalties.

After a short drive sipping my coffee, I pulled up to the gate of the private garage. The sensor read the sticker in my window, and the gate rose.

I drove in feeling fresh and clean, and parked in the same space I used every day. It's always available since I always arrive before anyone else, except Annette.

I put the emergency brake on, climbed out with my drink, and took the elevator upstairs to the third floor, which was the top floor of this architecturally beautiful building.

The Kinky Side of Perfect

"Good morning, Annette," I said as I walked by her office.

I could see her clearly through the wall of tempered glass, seated in her impressive office. She was poised at that cherry wood desk like a mad scientist queen, sipping Yerba Mate tea. Her eyes blazed with a passion for creating and a drive for nanoteching the world.

"Good morning mini-me. Are you passing thru or are you here working on a Sunday again, Roxanne?" she asked.

"You know me," I replied.

"Yes, I was you once. Remember? Keep that work ethic and you will get to this seat too." Annette said and smiled warmly before turning her full attention back to the stylish tablet computer perched in a cradle on her desktop.

I appreciated the nod and continued toward my desk feeling very validated.

CHAPTER 3

Another evening after work, Denise and I had plans to go shoe shopping. She met me at my place and we took her car. No need to burn gas with two vehicles, especially with the gas prices these days. She bought a pair of burnt orange strappy 6 inch heels lined with bling and I grabbed a pair of functional closed toe, navy blue pumps with insoles I could wear at the office. It took a little longer than expected to find the styles we were looking for, but it was a relief when we found them. And they had a buy-one-get-one half-off sale going on. Oh yes, our day was made.

Denise said, "What? For these prices? Girl, I got this. You can get the next one." I was grateful because my meager check from the lab only went so far anyway.

On the way back to my place, Denise said, "Ooh! I don't know how the time got away from me so fast. I have an 8:00 appointment online. It's too far to get home and still make it on time. Can I use your computer and wifi real quick when we get there? I have a little online meeting. You know how I do. Gotta let the suitors see me for real."

"I got you girl, of course," I said. Denise was a regional manager at a major restaurant chain and regularly had to attend long, dull teleconferences about the newest foccacia roll or whatever the latest trend was in fine dining at the time. She was good at her job though and had moved through the ranks quickly.

As soon as we stepped inside, she yelled through the house "Mr. Redman? Anybody here?" No one answered so we had the house to ourselves for a while.

We headed directly to my room and I set my purse down. I was beat. "I'm going to go shower," I told her. "You know the login and password. Help yourself." I said over my shoulder as I headed to the bathroom to turn the water on. I was happy to wash the lab and all that bargain hunting off for now. It had been an extremely long but productive day.

At the lab, we were close to a new discovery in our nanotech research, but that meant intense days. I enjoyed the shopping too and I loved my shoes but for now, I just wanted to relax and chill.

"Thank you, baby. Girl, go take your shower. I will be here online for one of my sessions when you come out," she said and started to log in.

As I was getting ready to come out of the bathroom, I heard Denise's voice saying, "You like that? Uh huh? Stroke that dick for me baby. I want to see all 10 inches of it. That's it. Ooooh..." I came to the door and peeked out. I could barely believe the freaky scene I was witnessing.

"What the hell?!" I said. She was still in her office clothes from her waist down but she had stripped down to her bra and had her breasts almost out in all their glory...almost. Denise always seemed to get off on flashing somebody. She leaned in to the webcam and shook her boobs into camera.

"That's it baby. That's it. You're almost there. Come on baby. Give me what I want daddy. Come for me. That's it. Oooh...That's it," she cooed into the camera.

I saw the man on the screen she was talking to. He was a wiry little man with extremely pale skin, thick glasses and grey hair that was sticking to his scalp from sweat. He sat in a banker's style plush maroon leather chair that made me wonder if he was broadcasting from an office in the financial district.

Even without clothes on, he could have passed for the stereotypical actuary. There he was, completely naked, sitting in a chair, and jacking off to my best friend, Denise. Then, like a rocket, he came and shot it up in the air with panache.

"Oh hell, no! No you didn't!" I yelled and stormed into the room. She must have been out of her mind to have done something like this. And at my house no less?

With his other hand, he grabbed a towel to wipe off and clean his hands. Then, he reached for the screen and tipped her an extra seventy five tokens for that happy ending. "Thank you, Dee Dee. You're the best," he said in a red-faced hurry and quickly logged off.

I was livid. "What are you doing?! Girl, you are crazy. I had an idea you were crazy before but now I know for a fact. Have you lost your mind?!" I said as I stared her in the face and slammed my laptop lid down.

"Lost my mind about what?" she said defiantly, while standing up, "I'm here in the comfort of my own home...well, technically your home. But either way it's a private place. Girl, you saw those tips. Other than the money, it feels like community service and you know I get off on serving the community."

"Yeah, the community and half of the high school football team. But this is different. And now they can get my IP address and possibly find out where I live! How dare you?" I demanded.

"I shoulda told you I was gonna be camming but I figured you would be in the shower so it wouldn't matter anyway. I love it. You should try it," she added flippantly as she slipped her breasts back into her shirt. "It might loosen you up a bit. Girl, you are so frigid, I bet your pussy is tighter than Fort Knox. Victor can probably barely get in there good. You need to relax and live a little."

"I'm fine thank you. I don't act like a cheap whore to feel sexy," I said but I regretted the words as they came out of my mouth.

"Look, don't get it twisted," she said while gathering the rest of her stuff. "Don't you dare confuse me with your sister. She worked the streets for years. That is a pro. This is different. I can't believe you're judging me right now. Part of the money I made online is how we got them shoes, so don't judge me. I mean, really. Really?"

"Sorry, Denise. It's just that, it's just... I never expected...You of all people...I...don't know what to say...", I stared at her like, who was this person I thought was my best friend?

"You know what?" she said, "You don't have to say anything. You can sit there and play miss high and mighty but you are no better than the rest of us."

"Denise, I..."

"Forget it. Bye. I'll see myself out," she said with a meanness usually reserved for serious enemies and walked out. "Hey, Candace," I hear her say to my sister as she passed by her walking down the hall.

She must have given me the side eye over her shoulder because I heard Candace ask, "What was that all about?"

"It's nothing," Denise told her. "You know your sister."

"Yeah girl, I know exactly what you mean," Candace said. "Alright later," she said.

As she passed my door, she looked in, rolled her eyes and let out a "Hmph." Then she kept walking to her room without saying another word.

See, Candace and I haven't gotten along lately either. As she walked by, I could tell she smelled like stale smoke and strong alcohol. Ever since she got clean 5 years ago when she got divorced and her kids were taken away, she stuck with plain cigarettes as far as I knew, and occasionally enjoyed her drink of choice but stayed away from the hard stuff.

Now, she worked the evening shift at the convenience store and went through her days like a zombie. It was better to keep our interactions brief and to the point.

To get over that whole thing, I headed to the kitchen and got a few scoops of that Mocha Almond ice cream. Then, I did a little busy work straightening up before making a light dinner of baked lemon pepper chicken, peas and roasted potatoes. I sat and ate like a robot in that empty dining room still in shock. Like, what the?

Man, this day couldn't have gotten any worse. I felt horrible.

CHAPTER 4

When I made it back to my room, I went to the closet to finish picking an outfit to wear the next day. I looked at the shoes she bought, put them back in the box, and stuck them way in the back of the closet on the floor behind all my other shoes. Then I remembered, I hadn't checked for any emails about some lab results from earlier in the day. I flipped open the screen and was greeted with my gorgeous all pink screen saver. I entered my password and logged in only to be greeted next with the site that Denise had been on.

I could barely get my mouse over to that "x" fast enough to close that screen. But once I closed that screen, another screen was behind it. I was about to x that one closed too when something caught my eye. This page was full of thumbnail images of other people who were broadcasting live like she had been. They were all in varying stages of undress. Women and men too. Whoa! I'd never seen that position before. I took a closer look.

I double-checked my webcam to make sure the little red light was off. That way, they couldn't see me. But just in case, I grabbed a tiny pink sticky note off the rainbow colored stack on my desk and stuck it over the lens.

Then, I remembered Candace was home so I jumped up and closed my door before taking a closer look at what I was seeing on the screen. So this was camming. Mmmm hmmm. Let me see what all the fuss was about.

The Kinky Side of Perfect

The first picture my eyes scanned to was of a naked freckled woman with her legs spread wide open. She was visible from the waist down only. Her pubic hair was red. She had a soft purple dildo in her hand and was stroking herself gently with it while moaning. Her location said she was broadcasting from the UK. Oh, this game was global like that? Alright.

I looked around at a few more of the pictures and saw a woman who appeared to be almost 80. I looked a little more closely. Yep. Her profile said she was 82. She was wearing a faded pink halter top with sequins. In one hand she held both a beer can and expertly balanced, rapidly burning cigarette. The other hand was reaching for her keyboard so she could chat.

If Denise were here, she would say, "Go ahead, granny. Get that money." I giggled at the thought. Then, I glanced over at her rising tips and saw that this woman was way ahead of Denise with that plan.

Another of the thumbnail videos was of a young couple who looked like they were in their mid-20s. When I clicked on the picture, their page opened to them in the middle of an affectionate kiss. I could see they were wearing wedding bands. A young married couple? What in the world would make them go on cam? Wasn't being on cam just for lonely, desperate, single people looking to get their rocks off or those who were seeking to get paid by any means necessary? Hmmm…

I looked at their details and saw they were broadcasting from Alaska. Then I saw that they were currently being viewed live, right now by 612 people. What? Who are these people watching? Who is this couple? Is this how they make their living?

Then they climbed on the bed and changed positions. OMG! Her rear end was full screen and was facing up in the air directly toward the camera. His hands firmly grabbed it and rocked it gently back and forth. I could clearly see his penis, which was fully erect, as he slid it in from behind. Caught in the heat of the moment, their moaning got louder.

Their camera was zoomed in so close, I could see her wetness flowing out with every long, slow thrust. She was cooing like it felt amazing. I rarely felt anything quite like that with Victor, so you know I was straight intrigued.

He stroked even faster and she said, "I'm coming. I'm coming!" All of a sudden, her body started shuddering and she moaned, "Ah!"

He said, "Yes. That's right." He supported her body as she came. Then, he flipped her gently over onto her back, kept the camera in the same position. With one swift stroke, he slid back inside and they moaned even more. He placed his hands lovingly supporting the back of her neck while he stroked slowly in and out.

Whooo...this man had skills. I should show this to Victor. Wait. What was I saying. I couldn't show this to him. What would he think? Or...maybe...we should watch it together? We could act out what we were seeing on the screen?

The scene on the computer drew me out of my daydream and back to the present. I heard him tell her, "I'm coming. Your good pussy feels so good. I love you. I love you!" He came deep inside her. The pleasure was evident on both of their faces.

After they relaxed a moment, he reached for his computer. The screen went blank and these words popped up on the screen "CammingCoupleOne has stopped broadcasting". I looked over at their tips to see how much they were making and realized they weren't accepting any tips. What? They must've been doing this for exhibition, purely because they wanted to. Interesting....

O...M...G... Now I have a better idea of what Denise was talking about and I owe her an apology. If that couple was any indication of what else I might find on this site, my mind was blown. Some were doing it for fun and it wasn't weird at all. I powered down my laptop and stared at the ceiling thinking about everything I'd just seen. Soon, my hand made it's way between my legs and I came intensely.

No shower head required.

CHAPTER 5

I woke up on the next day expecting to follow my usual morning routine. I worked out, got dressed, popped my phone in my purse, grabbed my keys, and went downstairs, but I was in for a pleasant surprise. The house was filled with activity. Mom had come back from her most recent assignment. Candace was already awake (what?!) and was helping her set the table in the dining room, and Dad was in the kitchen making breakfast.

"Hey Mom!" I smiled. We met halfway and hugged each other. "Welcome back."

My mother replied, "Thank you...thank God. Good to be home with you all, baby."

I knew by now not to ask her where she came from or where she goes, *ever*. She couldn't tell us anyway without losing her clearance.

My father walked in from the kitchen with pans of food.

"Good morning, Sunshine," Dad said. I gave him a kiss on the cheek.

"Hi Dad," I said with joy. The man was awesome.

"Hey Candace," I said, turning to my sister as I grabbed a piece of multi-grain toast from one of the platters and handed another to her. I was sincerely hoping there would be no drama from her this morning and was making my best effort to keep it peaceful. "Thanks," she said flatly, forcing a smile. Whoo, good. At least she's sober.

"I've got all of my special ladies here today, even if it's just for a little while," Dad said while he served scrambled eggs from the big iron skillet. I noticed the front page of the newspaper on the table. The headline read, "Legal Crusader Mitchell Jennings Brings Down Major Ring."

Jennings was a flamboyant attorney turned private investigator who often assisted local authorities in solving crimes - primarily to make himself look good. He was one of my Mom's magnet school classmates. After law school, he'd established his track record on some pretty high profile cases but it was obvious that he enjoyed spending a large part of his time in front of the press.

He set his sights on becoming a city councilman. Really, it seemed that his goal was to just be a public figure regardless of the office.

My parents, Tyler and Margaret Redman, have been married since they were highschool sweethearts. They'd had Candace when my Mom was 17. With both of my parents on the move so much, it always amazed me that they were even able to conceive me at all. But despite their frequent spells apart, my parents were always loving and considerate of each other when they were together. Clearly they were good for each other. From the look of us in a grocery store or in front of our beautiful suburban home, our family was picture perfect. But, no one was perfect.

Just then, though, we were there, me, my Dad, Mom, and sister, together at the same time, peacefully having breakfast on a weekday morning. This was a very special occasion indeed.

We made sure to savor it like we do all the happy times, especially when everyone was getting along.

Even though I had rarely seen my mother be affectionate with my Dad, that day, when he handed her the plate, she reached in and gave him a kiss on the lips. That rare public display of affection warmed my heart and made me smile. Plus, who really knew what sort of experiences Mom was carrying around in her after all of those times in the intense combat zones? I was glad to see her happy.

Only later did I realize then that their regular mode of a polite coolness instead of passion with each other had set the tone for my own relationships for years to come.

Determined to make it to the office on time, I told everyone I would see them later.

Mom said, "I will walk out with you, baby."

Once we reached the car, she asked me, "What's going on, sweetheart? You seem like you have a lot going on in that beautiful, brilliant noggin of yours."

I said to her, "I know your clearance won't allow you to say anything but sometimes I just wish I knew what your real life is like."

She stops me and interrupts saying, "You are my real life. You all are my real life."

I shook my head and said, "I love you mom but if you're somewhere else seventy percent of the time, that somewhere else is your real life. I'm not trying to hammer you over the head with this again, Mom, but what I'm really wondering is what your days like? What are your nights like in the places you sleep? Who are your friends? How well do they know you? I'm not judging you but I am just sharing some of the things I think about while you're away." I continued, "I want to ask your opinion on something."

"Let's hear it," she said.

I said, "Like you, I've spent a lot of years trying to be perfect. Don't you ever get tired of it? I am starting to notice that there may be more to life."

Never one to mince words, she asks me directly, "Are you cheating on Victor?"

"No!" I say laughing. "Why, are you cheating on Dad?"

She replied softly, not smiling, "If you were younger, I probably would tell you "no" and let you think that we have been monogamous all of our 39 years of marriage. That's just not the case. I have. He knows. He has. I know. Don't ask if you don't want the truth. We will save the details for another discussion. Just know this, your Dad and I are happy. We love each other very much. We have a situation that works for us." She continued, "Find a situation that works for you and don't be afraid to fail, fall, or look like an asshole. Just remember to do it with self-respect. I will always be proud of it no matter what. You've grown from a driven little girl, to an accomplished young woman, to a full-fledged force to be reckoned with. I couldn't be more proud of you. I would say that you could just ask any of the people in the field that I work with about it because I talk about you non-stop. But, you will just have to take my word for it."

She hugged me and smiled, "You're almost 35 now. Finally old enough to be President of this great country of ours. But first you give me some grandkids, then the Presidency," she teased. "But most of all, don't wait to be happy. I am going to love you no matter what. I don't expect perfection - just respect and discretion. We've already had enough family drama for a lifetime. I love your sister but…" she shook her head. "Fortunately, we raised you right. Thank you for three scandal-free decades. I trust your judgement. You've always been the level-headed one."

I hugged her back and climbed in the car feeling loved, uplifted, and refreshed. Although, I did have a few questions about Mom cheating on Dad, but like she said, he was happy and she was happy. That's all that mattered to me.

When I arrived at the office, I took a look around through the frosted glass at my cubicle trying not to be bored out of my mind. Generally, I loved what I did. Today, I wanted to be somewhere else. Everyone there was walking around in stark white lab coats, moving briskly about the office like slow moving oompa loompas in a sterile chocolate factory.

While I had always been an uber-geek, I still truly felt like an outsider among the swarms of techies and nerds in the main office. Perhaps it was a gender issue. I could not relate to a lot of their humor or interests.

I noticed a reminder on my calendar that there was a team meeting on the schedule. Shit. I was not in the mood. But you know me, if the meeting was called for 10am, I was there early. As I took my seat, I spoke to William Holtz, the guy with the highest IQ in the building, and one of the highest in the country. Generally, he was friendly and spent way too much time trying to convince us that he was just an everyday guy. Yeah, ok. He was always cool with me though.

After everyone else took their seats, Annette told all of us, "This is no place to play dumb. Like all of you, I know what it's like to have to go through life dumbing yourself down in order to avoid intimidating people. I went through a lot to get to where I am today. Here, I want you to brilliant yourself UP.

We can all help each other by creating a climate where genius is normal, accepted, and expected."

I swear she was looking at me on that last line, however, it was William who replied, "I understand, thank you for bringing us all together and providing this amazing opportunity."

I glanced over at William only to realize he wasn't being conceited, he simply had been told about his genius most of his life. Plus, he didn't have much experience when it came to social skills. He was just being himself.

It was then that I caught a glimpse of Bryce. He was staring at Annette in some type of way. As I looked back at her, I realized they held their gaze just a little too long.

On an ordinary day, Annette was the only person in the entire building with whom I could thoroughly identify. The generation gap did, however, play a role in some of the differences of opinions she and I had. That and a few million dollars. Yes, I had nothing but respect for Annette and gratitude for this job. With the exception of the office politics played by a few others, this was my dream job. I definitely would have had little patience for Bryce if he came by today, though, after the meeting.

I was so grateful that meeting wrapped up quickly. I politely said my good-byes and headed straight back to my desk for some peace. While waiting for some lab test results, my phone rang. I picked up the phone and was pleased to hear Victor's voice. I needed that right now.

We chatted and flirted quietly for a bit then it was back to going over my results for the recent lab tests. Something looked a little off. I needed to go over these results again, but later. Right then, it was time to feel that anticipation about seeing Victor.

Anyway, it was Tuesday, so when I left the lab, I would head directly over to his place where we would watch a movie, shower, then get in the bed and repeat the same familiar routine. At the end of the day, I called some of the lab team members to schedule a re-test of these results. They had to be not only right, but perfect in their findings.

Then, I headed over to Victor's. That evening, I had to let him know that I had a video chat call with my brother Everett scheduled for midnight. Based on my brother's hectic schedule wherever he was stationed overseas, that was the only time he could get a call in that week.

My brother Everett and I have always been close, way closer than Candace and I ever were because Dad started that trucking company when we were still young enough to be impressionable. That allowed us to have way more time together with our Dad. When Candace was growing up, he was still on the road and away from home most of the time which explained many of her whack issues but it's still no excuse.

So, for me and for Everett, Dad was always a strong influence in our lives. The whole family always had high hopes for my brother. He decided to join the Army right out of high school because it was the same branch of the military that Mom was in and that her Dad before her had served in. So for Everett, joining the military was the family business.

This was his third tour and I knew he missed everybody. The only way he could reach us was by screened mail which took forever or by a highly monitored video call. I was hoping he had a signal in his location because sometimes we could go for months without hearing from him at all.

As soon as I arrived at Victor's, I let him know about the call with Everett.

"Baby, that's fine," he said. "You know I will already be asleep. You're welcome to set up your laptop here in the living room if you like. That way he will be able to hear you and I will still be able to sleep ok, if he can still hear you over my snoring. Lol."

I giggled and teased him, "Yeah, you're right. I may have to close your room door to be able to hear him over that rattling."

"Is that right?" He smiled and pulled me closer to him. "Well, I am sure you are going to make it all worth my while before I even get a chance to start snoring. Mmm, " he took a step back and said, "Turn around for me. Girl you look good..."

"Thank you," I said demurely and turned around, twerking a little so he could get a good look at the curves.

"Oh...yessss. Alright. Ready to go to the market so we can grab a bite and hurry to get back, so we can get our evening started?" he asked.

"Sure. Let me just go to the little girls' room and I will be right out," I said.

As I headed down the hall, I enjoyed the light and the subtle warmth that was beaming down on me from the stylish track lights in the ceiling. When I got to the restroom, the toilet seat was already down. He was always so considerate. I swiftly finished, washed my hands, and went back to the living room.

"Ready," I said.

At the market, we grabbed some fresh salad with cucumbers, celery, and romaine lettuce. We also picked up some steak and sweet potatoes to bake. For dessert, I selected my favorite, chocolate cupcakes. Then, we headed back to his place to cook, eat, curl up on the couch, and watch a movie.

Here was how I would describe how I felt when I was with Victor. It wasn't bliss or blazing fires but at least it wasn't wife-beating, drunken, cussing drama either. It was middle of the road, just the way I like it.

I thought to myself as we curled up on the couch, "I really can see myself spending the rest of my life with this man. This feels safe, like home."

At about 10:00, I remembered the call with Everett and jumped up to prep for it in advance. I set up my laptop on the table in the living room, flipped the screen up, and plugged it in so it would be ready for the call.

Next, I left Victor on the couch, jumped in the shower, bathed and shaved. When I finished, I left the water running for him so he could jump in while I brushed and flossed my teeth. The movie was just about over anyway.

I lathered my body with cocoa butter lotion, spritzed on a little perfume, and slipped on a little white satin teddy with lace and a pair of matching white lace thongs.

I kept my feet bare because my French pedicure and French manicure were both still fresh from last Thursday's visit to the salon. When my legs are in the bed with him, my little tips and toes would shine like pearls.

I headed to the bed and did some light yoga stretches while he finished in the shower. Since I'd started that new self-defense class, my body was really feeling it. I breathed in deep and stretched from side-to-side to work those muscles out.

It was almost 11 when he emerged from the shower and was straight up looking like an Adonis. Muscles rippling. Body glistening. I could see that he was already hard. Plus, he was packing some length too. Thank you, Lord. And he was heading straight for the bed. He pulled back the edge of the blanket and climbed into the sheets. Laying on my side facing him, I slid the blanket down seductively and let him take a good look.

"Mmm, mmm, mmm," he said. "I am such a lucky man."

"Yes, you are," I replied as I traced my hand softly back up the side of my body letting the trim of my teddy slide up with my finger.

Nature took over and we were drawn to each other like magnets. I felt his lips on mine and they felt so, so good. I never wanted this kiss to end...He traced his lips down my body and slipped his thumbs in the hips of my thongs.

I squirmed gently because the pleasure of anticipation felt so strong. Maybe tonight would be different. Maybe tonight I can experience something like what I saw on the cams.

He slid my panties off and placed his tongue square between my legs. I could feel the heat of his breath on my clit. Then I felt his tongue. Oh yes. He licked nice and slow. Then again, a little deeper this time. Then, he licked from the opening all the way up past my clit like he's licking the side of an ice cream sandwich. It...felt...so...good.

Then, he slid up and circled his dick around inside my pussy lips. I shuddered and threw my head back totally relaxed. Looking down between my legs, I watched it as he slid it in. First the head, then all the rest.

My body instantly responded and my legs opened wider to make space for his dick as it slid into my wet pussy. He slid it out halfway then thrust it in gently even deeper. I dug my fingers into his back and held on to him. It...was...so...long.

He let out an "ahhhh!" and he came intensely... Yes, it was just that fast. He kissed my lips and slid out slowly, then went to the bathroom to wash up, and got back in the bed. He gave me a goodnight kiss adoringly, slipped on that mask, turned on his side facing away from me, and he was out. Gone. Snoring.

I headed to the shower but tonight I kept my eye on the clock. It was already 11:44.

I showered again quickly, no time to lounge this time. I threw on one of Victor's business shirts with a pair of my jeans and headed into the living room. I clicked on the computer, entered my password, and waited.

At exactly 12:00, the computer beeped with the video call. I answered, "Hey, hey little bro."

"Hey sis. What's good?" My brother Everett looked tired but I know there was nothing he could tell me about why he was exhausted or what was happening. So, I asked him something basic. "How's the food?" He laughed.

"Good," he said, "Not as good as Dad's though. How's he doing?"

"He's good," I told him. "Everything's good. Busy running his business. You know how that is. Mom's back for a while. She looks great. Strong and aloof as ever. But seems a little warmer toward Dad lately. I'm liking what I'm seeing there."

"And Candace?", he asked hesitantly.

"She's... Candace. For now, she's at the house and everybody's getting along. It's been awhile since she went to see Tony, and the kids. Can you believe little Anthony is eight already? And Jemma is going to be six? Honestly, though, I wonder if she's ever going to get partial custody of the kids back. I can't believe it's been five years since she lost those kids 'cause of her yo-yoing in and out of rehabs. Right now, even though she's clean, she's still walking around zombified, like she was when you came to visit last time. Maybe it is the best thing for the kids to stay with their dad until they are eighteen. At least he's giving them a pretty stable life."

"Tony's a good guy," he said. "Man, I remember when they first got together. I was happy for them. Happy that she finally found love after all that drama but I don't know if he realized all of what he was getting himself into. I am glad he's there for the kids. So what about you? What's up?"

"Yep. It's Tuesday. I'm over at Victor's."

"Yeah, it is Tuesday where you are, huh?" he said reflectively.

"All day today," I replied.

"So, uh, wedding? Am I getting some more nieces? Nephews? What's up? I mean, dude is a little bland for my taste, but I like him for you!" He laughed which is good. I can see he needs it.

I shooshed him a little bit, "He's asleep in the next room." I thought about it and smiled, "I do enjoy him though. Yeah, we are good. Taking it one step at a time."

"Redman!" I heard someone bark to him in the background.

"Ok, sis. Gotta go. Love you. Tell everyone I said hi and I'm good," he said.

"I will," I said. "Love you, too." He signed off. I sighed and leaned back on the couch. It was good to talk with him but I worried about him sometimes. I would be glad when he is back home safe.

Thinking about what he had said, was now was the time for the van, the kids, and the picket fence? Was I ready for all that? I heard Victor snort in his sleep from the other room then go back to his deep rattle of a snore. I grabbed a pillow and hugged it for a second, wondering if this was a sneak preview of my whole future.

CHAPTER 6

The computer was already open. I made sure Victor was still asleep. He was. I turned back to the screen and opened an incognito window.

I typed in the url. No need to check the history this time. I knew it by heart now. Oh yeah, I almost forgot the mute. Hit that. Okay, good. Now, it was time to browse. It was then that I noticed there were different tabs: featured, female, male, couples, and trans. They had something for everyone.

First, I clicked to "Females" to see who was doing what. The first one was a 19 year old woman from Columbia. Her profile said she was interested in Men, Women, Trans, and Couples. Evidently, she was an equal opportunity service provider. Her nails were cute though. They were a fiery orange and contrasted nicely with her blue bikini top which was pulled down so her nipples were showing. She was rubbing a dildo on her private area and she had something small and pink stuck in her rectum. She was gyrating with her legs spread open to the camera. On the right, I could see that she was getting tips. In fact a username MasterDeliciousness just tipped 10 tokens. Ok.

I went over to the "Males" tab. Wow. All those faces. They all looked so vulnerable. Some were cute. And these penises. I had never seen so many types, shapes, and sizes. OMG. I clicked on one named Rico who was wearing his pants buttoned up but had his fly open and his penis out, swinging. I look over at the chat window. Yep. He was getting tips too. BBallzz chats for Rico to show his balls. Rico continues to let it swing. Then BBallz tips 5 tokens. All of a sudden, Rico reaches in his pants and whips out two enormous testicles.

Always organized, I continued down the line in order. Next was the "Couples" tab. I looked back again at Victor. Yeah, he was still out. Ok, the first one was of a woman bent over, shown from behind. She had something pink and skinny sticking out her pussy. When she bent over, it stuck out like a little tail. I thought this was supposed to be couples. Where was her man? Next.

Some of these faces were so distinct. Some had on masks like they didn't want to be recognized. Others had their full face and their legs open to the world. There was another couple KissiKam. Hey, she had that same pink thing stuck inside her pussy. What was that? At least her man was there with her. Someone tipped 20 tokens and she moaned a "thank you."

Her man caressed her nipples from behind while sitting on the bed. Then, he stood up and sat in the chair in front of her. She obediently got on her knees and proceeded to suck his dick. Someone else tipped 10 tokens and she looked down between her legs and moaned again. I noticed in the hashtags in the chat, I kept seeing the word #RealTimeTipAVibe.

After some research, I found out how the TipAVibe worked. It was a wireless bluetooth vibrator that was stimulated by tips from users. Every time they tipped, the device would vibrate and stimulate the cam model. This was some space age shit.

I went back to their tab and someone named Sterling just tipped them one token. The vibrator went off in her pussy while she was on her knees with his dick in her mouth. She moaned while trying to swallow his dick. This was almost sensory overload.

I flipped to another couple called FaceKissing. She had a dog collar on and her hands were bound behind her back. Her boyfriend was reading the chat window taking instruction from the people who were giving the tips. He pulled out a ball gag and slipped it in her mouth. She giggled the whole time. He pulled out a leather paddle and hit her on the ass. It made a red circle. She yelped, then giggled some more.

He leaned in, read the screen, and said "Ok baby. There are tips for four more hits." Spank. Spank. Spank. Spank.

She mouthed "thank you" even through the ball gag and giggled some more. Whew! It took all kinds.

I headed over to "Trans". Amazing. KhloeB had a dollface and was wearing a blue negligee. Panties were pulled down to reveal a fully erect penis. I looked over at the chat. PearlxJam tipped 25 tokens and requested "ass plz". KhloeB rolled over, ass in the air and smiled.

Folks were on there getting their money. I went back to look up the TipAVibe to see where they sold them. Maybe I could use one on nights that I wasn't with Victor. Not on cam of course but maybe some kind of vibrator or something?

I looked up a couple of the local adult shops and noted the addresses. One of them was not too far from the office. I logged off and powered down the computer. I curled up under the blanket and made myself cum. I was blossoming sexually and developing a taste for more. I went to the bathroom and washed up. Then I slipped in the bed and looked over at Victor.

Where do we go from here? Should I tell him? Would he watch with me? Probably not. Yeah, he was super, suuuper traditional. Forget it. On the surface, we had a good thing going. Why rock the boat?

CHAPTER 7

The net morning, while sitting in the car behind my tinted windows right after parking in the employee garage, Bryce's Land Rover sped around the corner and screeched into a parking space one row away. His windows were wide open and I could hear the Ready To Rock You song blasting from his speakers but I could also hear giggling coming from the car even though I didn't see anyone else in the car. He cut the engine and the music went silent. The giggling went silent too as he moaned and leaned his head back in the driver's seat.

Then, he reclined his seat all the way back and climbed into the backseat. His passenger popped up and joined him in the back. OMG! It was Annette's executive assistant, Patricia, who at 5'9" in flats, 260 plus, Hawaiian Samoan, and black belt certified also doubled as her bodyguard and personal concierge.

Patricia had a beautiful face, rich golden skin, long black hair, and the generous curves that men have worshipped for centuries. Yet, her sheer mass and serious face had a tendency to intimidate a large percentage of men. But not Bryce. Right then, he was bowed down, worshipping at the altar as she reclined flat on the back seat with her hot pink painted toe nails pointed up in the air.

I slouched a little lower in my seat to make sure they couldn't see me at all. It was early so the garage was pretty quiet and inactive otherwise. How in the world could they not be more careful? But then again, perhaps they wanted to be seen.

He climbed on top of her, pulled a condom out, and began putting in work, right there in the garage. He was saying all kinds of things like,"Who's your Daddy's" and "Give me that sweet pussy." I knew this man had skills.

Next, I heard him say, "I'm coming. I coming! Oh, fuck! Yes!" and he came with intensity. He reached back up and slicked his hair back in place then he climbed off of her.

She reached down, slid the condom off, and said sexily, "I can get rid of this for you, baby."

He couldn't snatch that condom out of her hand fast enough. He told her, "Ah, ah, ah. You say that every time. We've been doing this for a few months now and you still have to ask. My mom told me about that little trick when I hit puberty. Do you know how many women would kill to have a Clarke heir?"

Patricia smirked softly and batted her eyes innocently, "Who me?".

He laughed and rolled his eyes playfully, "Yeah, honey. I know what time it is. Speaking of the time. I believe…."

Patricia cut him off and handed him a manila folder. "Here's a little dirt, some hot tea on most of the management in the office, for your mischievous delight, you naughty man, you," she said flirtatiously, adjusting her bra and massive boobs.

Like most of Annette's core team, Patricia was also ambitious. The Bone Bryce Club was the special sorority mostly made up of the interns who had joined the firm over the past 6 months that Bryce had been at this location of the company. Patricia knew better. She must have another agenda. I wondered if he saw it. Based on the way his eyes rolled back, he probably couldn't see shit, except the freaky thoughts going through his mind as she slobbed his knob so skillfully.

Patricia reached in the front seat and grabbed her bag. She then opened the back door and climbed out. "Are you gonna come in?" she asked.

"I'll be in in a minute," he said. "We don't want to start any tongues wagging by walking in together do we? I'm going to take a minute and get myself together. Then, I will be right up."

"Alright. See you inside, handsome," she said as she winked.

As soon as she closed the door, he reached for his phone and made a call. Will this man hurry up? I was ready to get to my desk without being noticed. And my coffee was getting cold.

All of a sudden, the door to the building opened and the security officer from the day shift came out. He walked over to Bryce's car and handed him a thumb drive through the back window. He'd been recording his sessions all along. This man is way more scandalous than I thought. Now I really had to watch my back. The officer took some bills from Bryce and gave him a fist pound.

"Another one for the archive, huh?" the guard asked.

"Yo player, that's why they call me the ladies man, dog. Watch and learn, homie." Bryce said.

They both laughed and the officer headed inside. Then, Bryce grabbed his things and headed in. Just as he was about to step through the door to the building, my phone vibrated with a text. Oh shit!

Bryce must have heard it and stopped in his tracks. With those sneaky eyes, he scanned the garage. Then, he straightened his posture, brushed his shoulder off, and headed inside. I guess he realized, *so what if someone had seen him*? He was THE Bryce Clarke and they couldn't touch him anyway. That MF.

I looked down at my phone and read Mom's text that she was headed back out of town. Well, at least it was good to see her at breakfast. It was great actually since those times were so few and far in between. I realized I better get in the office. I grabbed my bags and headed in as discreetly as I could.

Denise would have loved to hear this story. She was always telling me that I should fuck Bryce or any "upper caste" free male or female for the sole sake of corporate advancement. Oh, that was so not happening. That was exactly why I kept Denise away from certain people in my circle. She would have slept with Bryce herself if she had the chance, or even Victor. She was my homegirl and all but I wouldn't trust her around my man, my brother, or even my dad. But I still love her. She has rolled with me through a lot.

Man, I have gone all these years without seeing too much, and now I am seeing some of the freakiest stuff I have seen in my life.

I must have been PMSing because for some reason, that day the loud hum and bluish glare of the florescent lights in the lab seemed especially harsh. Just when I thought things couldn't get more hectic, an emergency meeting was called. I noticed my buddy, William Holtz, was missing. Before I could ask anyone about him, Annette rushed in with flourish.

She began, "By now some of you have heard." She put the back of her hand to her forehead. "It turns out that William has been falsifying his results."

Gasps echoed across the room.

Annette continued, "These results were directly responsible for his swift rise with the company as well as the reason for his hasty exit." She squinted her eyes and scanned the team members carefully. "If I find out that any of you were involved...Well you know the rest. You can kiss your cushy bonuses and your lives in this business goodbye. You will be dead to me. Now, moving forward, if you are noticing any discrepancies in your findings or any unusual results, you come to me *immediately*. Or that is YOUR ass on the line, not mine. I have worked too hard and sacrificed too much to establish this pristine top industry standing we have today..." she paused to survey the room once more before walking out and added, "and I intend to keep it."

I could barely believe it. Not William. He reminded me of Stephen Hawking in the vastness of his ideas and a revered saint with his ethics. What was going on? There had to be some mistake. As I walked back to my desk, I thought back to my own findings and reconfirmed the time and date for our team meeting to go over them again. They had to be correct now. There was no room for error.

I realized too that there may have been some logical cause to the error in William's results. Between racing thoughts over today's meeting and my personal life, time flew by. I looked up and most of the folks had already gone. I was one of the last ones in the office...again. I packed up to leave but just before leaving, I headed to Annette's office to ask her to give William a chance to explain.

As I approached, I stopped before I became visible through her glass office walls because I could hear voices. The door was just cracked open so I could hear clearly and see a little inside when I peeked.

Annette was talking to Bryce. Him again?

Annette said, "You know, Bryce. I feel like I can trust you. So I will confide in you that William and I were having an affair…But in light of what's happened, I had to let him go professionally and from my private life."

I waited for his reaction but there was none.

She crossed the room to be closer to him and continued, "Bryce, I am going to speak frankly. As Nicholas' son, you have a very special place in this company and in my heart. I have seen how you are with the ladies. Now is as good a time as any for me to join the Bone Bryce Club and bring a whole new experience to its ranks. What do you have to say about that?"

He raised his perfect brow as he said, "I was wondering when you'd ask, Annette. You've known our family most of my life. Growing up, my friends and I placed bets on who would get you in bed first when we got old enough."

Annette purred and laughed, "I knew you little horny motherfuckers were up to no good. Either way, I'm glad to hear that you are open to the idea. So let's make it official. As of right now, you are mine. That means no more fucking around with any of the other women, except me. Tomorrow morning, I will need you to go and get your STD tests and bring me a clean bill of health as soon as it is ready. By the way," she paused dramatically, "I know your dirty little secret."

Bryce said feigning innocence, "What are you talking about?" Regardless of what it was, he already knew he was guilty.

Annette said victoriously, "I have eyes and ears everywhere. I follow your every move. Even that security guard that brings you the recordings of your…indiscretions is on MY payroll. The point is this. I know that you tampered with William

Holtz's results and got away with it. Aaaand, I also that know that that is exactly the type of man I need by my side as we rise in the ranks among these sharks in the industry."

"Well, Annette," Bryce said probably relieved that someone understood him 100%, "I am glad we can come to this agreement."

Then, they moved into a small alcove across the room, away from the main view of a casual passerby, but I could still see their reflection in the glass. They embraced for a moment and then Annette gently pushed Bryce's head down until he was on his knees. With overly expert hands, he slid her skirt up to her waist.

He then started licking between her legs like an obedient lap dog. She took her hands, put them on his head, and buried his face in even deeper. I tiptoed to get a closer look and kept watching.

She said, "Oh yes, that's it" and threw her head back in pleasure while he worked. He slid her leg open wider. He hooked her thong with his thumb and eased it to the side gently rubbing it on her clean shaven lips and swollen clit. He proceeded to suck even more. Now I could see why the women in the office were so sprung.

Then, he grabbed her hips and spun her around so she was facing the wall. He caressed her hair, unleashed the bun, and positioned himself for penetration. He took a condom from his wallet and rolled it on. Ever so slowly, he kissed her on the back of her neck, flipped her hair over to the front, and slid in slowly. Annette moaned loudly.

I could hear him saying, "Who's the boss now? Who?"

"You are. You are. Oh, yes...." she managed to get out between breaths and moans.

I stood watching for what felt like a good 10 minutes just processing all of what was happening today. I looked down and saw that my nipples were standing at attention through my blouse. Ok, I'd seen enough. I tiptoed quietly on the carpet back past my desk and went out the other exit, closing the door as quietly as I could.

On the way to the car, I was trying to process all of what I was feeling. It was a combination of surprise, horniness, and astonishment at the lengths to which people will go when they go after something they want. Man, there was no use talking to Annette about William. He was a casualty of her personal agenda and taken down by her minion, Bryce.

Oh, shit...This added a whole other level to the sugar daddy game. Or was it sugar mama? Or really, who was using who? They both had something to gain. Man, blind ambition was real. I thought to myself that I needed to keep my head down when it came to Annette *and* Bryce or I could be next.

Slippery ass Bryce could fabricate false results with my own research or sabotage me or my work. I realized at that moment that I would probably have to accept one of his fake requests to be on one of his teams, a.) to avoid any fallout due to his alliance with Annette and b.) keep friends close but keep enemies...well you know the rest. Fuck!

Totally deflated by today's events, I needed to call someone I trusted. I needed to talk. NOW. When I got to the safety of my car, I took out my phone discreetly and dialed.

"Hey girl. Yes?" Denise asked when she picked up the phone.

I really needed her more now than ever. "I was calling to apologize," I told her and continued, "Girl, I don't know what is going but I needed someone to talk to."

"Umm, hmm. I bet you do," she replied.

I knew better than to talk about what just went down at the office while I was still in the building or while on the phone because I knew everything was being recorded. Plus, we all were required to sign a non-disclosure agreement as a stipulation when we were hired. I wanted to keep my job.

On the other hand, we could chat about her life freely. First of all, because she didn't work there, but primarily because she had no shame. So, on the ride home, I sincerely apologized to her and we spoke openly, real talk. I was happy to get my mind off of work for a moment.

We chatted for a while until we were back on good terms, like always. It was then, she told me the whole juicy story that she hadn't shared with anyone else about how she got started camming.

She had been a cam model for a while. One of our mutual friends had gotten her into it. The friend told Denise that she could make a little money on the side and didn't even have to leave her house. All she had to do was smile and talk to people on the webcam. She could strip a little if she wanted or go all out nude with it. Basically, she could do whatever she liked, and make even more. Plus, the friend got a little commission for every new person she signed up on the site.

Denise said that she was a natural. She inherently understood the psychology of her viewers and catered to every sort of fantasy that came her way. For the ones who wanted a dominatrix, she dressed up for that and even had a full size whip that she would crack. For the ones who had a foot fetish, she would put on her highest stripper heels and feature her feet on screen. Even for the ones who wanted to be insulted or even blackmailed, she did that and did it exceptionally well.

I said, "Blackmail?"

She had said, "Girl, yes. That is the hottest trend right now. They love that shit. For those that want that self-deprecating talk, I got that, too. Seems like the meaner I act towards them, the more they tip. Go figure."

By then, I was curious. "How does it actually work and how much money do you actually make?" She always had the hottest designer bags and phone accessories.

Denise teased, "Uh huh. Why don't you go to my page and cam anytime you want. Then you can see firsthand how much I make. Just split them tips with me, 50/50."

"Ha ha," I had replied sarcastically, "Very funny."

I had to hand it to her though. Those tips from a pure mathematical perspective were way more than what I was making at the lab. Plus, just merely talking with her about camming reminded me of all I'd seen that turned me on.

My mind wandered back to the cam sites and the sensations that had warmed my body as the horniness increased. I thought for a second what it might be like to really be on cam, to strip for strangers and bare the most intimate parts of my body for the world to see. Ooh, the mental images that came to mind. What would my family say?

But then again, who had to know it was me? I could hide my face, or not show it on cam, or I could even disguise myself. Then, I would be free to cam and do what I wanted, when I wanted.

"Anyway girl, I just wanted to say I'm sorry," I told her.

"No worries, girl. I still got love for you, even if you are the original ice princess, hoity toity, and the whole nine. I can look past all that."

I laughed, "Yeah, whatever. Later," and we hung up.

I grabbed a quick burrito from the drive-thru in a hurry to get home and pick up where I had left off on the computer the previous night. My leg tapped in nervous anticipation.

CHAPTER 8

As soon as I got home, I took my laptop and carefully carried it out to what I called my personal lab. This lab was more like an old tree house the size of a storage shed which sat in the yard on the ground just behind the main house. Dad built it for me by hand years ago and the structure still looked like a beautiful mini Victorian dollhouse even after all these years.

The deep red paint was peeling a little and the white shutters were worn with wear from the elements, but it still looked regal. More importantly, it did the job when it came to finding privacy.

I spent hours out there on the regular. So, my family was used to it. It was my "go to" place to do homework, cuddle up with a book, or take some "me" time. Back when Candace was wilding out, I started the habit of slipping out here to find some peace.

Once safely inside, I sat down at the desk and flipped the laptop open.

I took off my work clothes, slipped on my red super-soft satin kimono robe that I usually used for reading. Then, I put the sticky note over the camera on my computer and settled in to watch privately. Over time, I became a little familiar with some of the different sites and even began to recognize some of the cammers by their screen names or faces.

The Kinky Side of Perfect

After a few weeks of watching, I decided maybe it was time to take the sticky note off. I would still hide my face though. They could see my robe and that was alright, right? Even so, anonymity was the way to get started in this game. Others got in, made their loot, and got out. Seemed harmless enough.

It was time to turn my cam on. I adjusted my camera and made sure they couldn't see my face. I took a deep breath, went to one of the cam sites, set up a profile under NewNewbie007, and clicked the "start broadcasting" button. This way, other people could see me, or my robe rather, as I browsed their pages. As soon as I started the broadcast, I look up at the screen and there was somebody watching me already! I quickly clicked "stop broadcast".

Look, Roxanne, I told myself, this was not the time to be shy. To calm down, I grabbed a little liquid courage, a tiny bottle of champagne I'd gotten in a favor bag from a wedding last year, and drank half of it down. That took the edge off. I sat back down and clicked the "start broadcast" button.

Once again, someone started viewing right away. Then another. They were literally watching me as I sat there and just browsed the other videos in my robe. Some tried to communicate with me on chat but I didn't answer any of them. I just watched and saw one scene after another, one position after another. Oh, man. This was amazing. I glanced at the clock on my screen and realized that 2 hours had gone by. Time had just flown. Enough for today. I logged off.

At work the next day, people were still walking on eggshells after that whole William debacle. I may have been the only one who knew the real truth. I was sure glad Annette was on my side because I realized that she was ruthless, just like Bryce. She might do anything just to get ahead. Is that how I had to be to make it in the biotech world?

I had an electronic lock put on the specific lab where we were working on my current project and gave only the key team members the code. I was so glad Bryce wasn't one of them. Before leaving the office that evening, I made sure all doors and my desk drawers were locked tight and that there was nothing important left out on my desk except the plant and my phone.

The days were starting to fly by. While work was my life for years, now, it just didn't seem as important. My time at the office seemed shorter as if all that mattered was getting home to watch. Even more, some part of me was looking forward to being seen.

As soon as I got to the sanctuary of my home that evening, I logged on. I was finally getting a little nerve. I still broadcasted showing just my robe, but this time, I decided to accept tips and chat with a few of the viewers just for fun. The first dude's screen name was SuperrrdudeT. He tipped a few tokens. This was great! He tipped one token at a time and just dragged the time out. Eventually, his conversation was so boring, I had to stop chatting with him. I just let him watch. My time was better spent browsing. I appreciated his tips though.

The next one I chatted with that popped up had the screen name KokDeisel. He seemed cool enough. I checked his profile. He was on but he had his face hidden, too. We had some pretty clever conversation and he kept me laughing. He sprinkled some tips in too here and there. We chatted for the time I was on and said we'd pick it up the next day. When we wrapped it up, he tipped an extra 25 tokens.

When I logged back on that next day, I convinced him to let me see a pic. At first, he was hesitant but then he let me see his face. He looked like he was fresh out of college and looked like a surfer or something!

I quickly logged off from his room. I was waaay too young to be feeling like somebody's cougar already. It was kind of disappointing, though. Our convos were great.

I chatted with a few more, loving the attention and the tips. One guy came on and tipped right away. We started chatting. We flirted a little but then I took a look at his profile. Wait! Was that my neighbor? Oh shit! It was! Chatting with me was one my neighbors, Mr. Phillips, sitting right there, naked, plain as day, in that easy chair in his office I had seen so many times visiting over the years during holiday parties and graduations.

He typed, "Oh my God, I see you're a Carrolton Lion. I went to that school. What year did you graduate?" He tipped 10 more tokens.

Oh shit! I looked behind me and saw one of my old yearbooks sitting on a shelf behind me. Mr. Phillips continued to jerk off while typing in the chat box. I slammed the off button for the whole computer.

I so hope he did not recognize me or anything else in the background that could help him put two and two together. I jumped up and snatched that yearbook off the shelf. I stuffed it under some old Cosmo and S2S magazines making sure that it couldn't be seen. I scanned the room to see if there were any other identifiable items. Cool. I was good.

This was getting waaaay too close to home. Plus, I didn't need to see him in all his glory. I would never look at him the same way when I saw him out there doing the yard.

That was enough for me. I was not doing this anymore. The whole thing was too risky, anyway. I had always been very risk adverse. Denise was the one to take risks. I, on the other hand, was done.

I called Denise. Thank goodness she picked up.

"Hey girl, what it do? What it do?" she asked loudly into the phone.

"Girl, let me ask you something. Have you ever seen anyone you know when you are on cam?" I asked.

"Girl, please. I have seen everybody. I've seen my neighbors, them people at the grocery store, my Sunday school teacher, and even my P.O. Why do you ask? Never mind. I know you can't talk about nothing on the phone. Anyway, fuck all this cyber stuff. We need to get back to the real world. I got VIP passes to Deja Blue compliments of my dude DJ Boy Toy for tonight. You are coming. I will be there to pick you up two hours. Better make it an hour. I know to throw in the extra hour for make-over time to correct whatever conservative outfit you got on and make it hot."

"Ha ha. Yeah. I love you too. See you in an hour," I said.

It was good to break the homebody routine every now and then. Especially after seeing Mr. Phillips, I definitely needed to do something to clear my mind.

I packed my laptop up and vowed to use it only for work and email from now on. I felt like I had to get control of my life back. Normally, I found great comfort in my routines and what was happening with me was anything but routine.

Denise came by to pick me up. I squeezed into a tight red dress she brought over and I had to admit, it looked great. In the car, I filled her in on what had been happening with the cams. All she had to say was, "Go 'head, girl. I told you there was another world out there." She was right.

When we got to the club, we bypassed the line and headed straight for the VIP entrance. Once we got inside, I could see

69

men, women, men dressed like women, women dressed like men, and everything in between. Compared to the office, it was like being transported to wonderland. Plus, the music was amazing.

I heard over the mic, "My girl D-D-Denise in the house!"

Denise walked me straight over to the DJ booth where I met Boy Toy. He was about 6 feet, slim, with jet black hair swept up like a lead singer from a boy band. He was definitely a little quirky like Denise and I could see why they were friends. He was like a mad genius back there working those digital turntables. He introduced us to the guy standing next to him as his boyfriend, Ross. We chatted it up a little while he spun and then we headed to our VIP booth where there was already champagne waiting for us. The hostess poured us a couple of glasses and we raised a toast to DJ Boy Toy.

This man knew how to hype up a party. But even more importantly, Denise knew some amazing people. I was having a great time. We partied and danced in VIP for a while then ventured out to the main dance floor. A couple of guys asked us to dance.

Denise said, "Here, you take the cute one. You need to relax. Forget all about Victor and the cams for a minute. Go!"

He and I danced. Then later, she and I danced, just having fun, enjoying life.

After a couple of drinks, I was feeling a little tipsy, so we headed back to VIP to chill and enjoy the music. Denise teased me about getting drunk off a tiny bit of champagne. I wasn't drunk, though. I just felt uninhibited.

At about 1:30, the guest DJ went on. So, DJ Boy Toy and Ross came over to join us. We all sat in the booth and chatted it up. Denise started telling them some of my cam stories.

"Denise!" I said, "Don't tell anybody. That was for your ears only!"

"Girl, chillax. They are cool. They know I do it and he used to do it too."

DJ Boy Toy said, "Oh yeah. Some of the things I've seen...and done." He and Ross laughed.

Feeling reassured, I said, "Well, in that case, it's not just the things I've seen but some of the things I wish I could unsee." Everybody laughed at that one.

"Talk to us. What is it?" Boy Toy asked.

I told him about some of the categories. He knew them all. Then I told him about some of the tips.

He replied, "Yeah, that's how I got some of my early DJ equipment."

Denise teased him, "You didn't tell me that!"

He said, "I didn't know you were camming back then."

Ross said, "I knew. In fact, I helped him moderate the chats. I would hide my face though or wear a mask, glasses, or a fake beard or something so people wouldn't know it was me. Some of my favorite times were throwing people out of the room when they got too rowdy, making demands."

Denise said, "I am learning all kinds of stuff tonight about this crew. Mm hmm, and you all tell me I'm the freaky one."

"You are!" We said in unison. The table laughed again.

"Uh huh, y'all just jealous 'cause I make more than half my income from it."

"Oh good!" Boy Toy said. Then he stood up and said aloud, "Drinks on Denise!" He sat back down, "Just kidding!" We all laughed again.

We chatted for awhile more, then at about 2:00am Denise noticed the time.

"Girl, we gotta go. I have an early appointment with a buyer at one of the restaurants."

We all said our good-byes and she and I headed out. Boy Toy told us we were welcome to come back anytime. That hanging out with us was a highlight of the night for them. While I was tipsy, Denise was not, so she could drive home.

On the way home, still in a relaxed state, I looked up at the stars as we rode. It was great to be out of my skin for a while.

I thought back on camming said to Denise, "It may be ok for you all but I'm done. Seeing Mr. Phillips was the icing on the cake."

Denise said, "It's your decision. But me? I'm gonna do it as long as I can. Make it rain. Make it rain!"

We laughed and talked all the way back. When she dropped me off and I told her a sincere thank you for getting me out of the house.

"Girl, you good. Get some rest," she said and drove off. I walked inside. I was quiet. I showered and went to sleep, happy with my decision to leave cams alone.

CHAPTER 9

The next week at work was like every other. Office politics. People in white lab suits. At least our research was going well. My mind kept wandering to the cams though. They provide an extra excitement to my lives. I felt like I was peering into their lives when I watched and seeing how the people on camera lived. It felt very intimate, like they were exposing themselves fully to anyone who logged on. Part of it was fascinating. They looked like they just wanted some company. Someone to love them.

I tried to stay away from the cams but I was torn. I wanted to leave them alone but something inside me just couldn't. It was dominating my thoughts, even at work, and even while I was at Victor's. The cam images kept luring me back in. I found all sorts of ways to justify why it might be okay if I did just a little camming and figured that I could do it without any repercussions.

First and foremost, if I did cam again, I was going to need a bit more camouflage than just hiding my face. So, that Saturday night, on the way home from work, I stopped by the beauty supply and picked up a bright red wig, heavy make-up and some super long lashes. Anyone who knew me in real life would know that the real Roxanne Redman would never wear those.

Once I got home and went to the lab, I slipped that wig on. Reading the instructions on the back of the eye lash package, I put those lashes on. Then, I applied the make up in the style that the back of the package called a full smokey eye.

I took a long look in the mirror. Whoa! Who was that?! I looked nothing like myself. Candace wouldn't even recognize me. I felt fully empowered. Now, I could be WHOEVER I wanted to be. That feeling was liberating in a way I could barely describe. It was as if I gave myself an "all access" pass to my own life. I still kept the camera tilted down so they couldn't see my face, though.

That night, I logged on more confident than ever. Plus, after last night with the neighbor, who knew what I was going to see? Fortunately, I was in for a pleasant surprise. This dude, screen name Sterling G, popped up in my chat window.

"Hey," he typed in the chat window in my room. "Your body is gorgeous."

I wondered if that was the same Sterling who tipped that couple before. I opened another tab, clicked on his user profile, and saw that he was a 40 something, slim, cafe mocha colored guy with glasses. Feeling flirty, I spoke and typed, "You can see all that through this thick robe?"

"Dayummmm…you got a sexy voice, too," he says. "Can you lean over a little. I want to see more of that fine body." He licked his lips and leaned closer to the screen to get a better look. I arranged both tabs so our screens were both up side by side.

My nipples immediately went to attention because it was like I could feel his lust through the screen. It made me feel a little shy, too, since this was my first time somebody was commenting on my body directly. So, I slid my chair a little farther away from the screen and leaned the back of the laptop down a little farther to make sure he could not see my face.

He says, "Wait, wait. I'm really lonely. My wife left me. I'm really stressed out at work. I really just need someone to talk to. You look like you're kind of lonely and need someone to listen to what you're going through. Am I right?"

For a second, I was about to log off, but he seemed harmless enough. Plus some other people had logged on to watch me too.

"Yeah, you're right," I answered him honestly. I'm glad it's anonymous. Might as well have somebody to talk to. Just like sitting at a bar or a coffee shop right?

Before I could say something else, I heard that ringing like a Vegas slot machine.

He says, "Look, I just tipped you 100 tokens. Just to talk. Please. Will you talk to me? I just need some company. There's nobody else I can talk to. You keep the money. Just talk. I swear."

I thought, a hundred just to talk? This must be the easiest money ever. I closed my robe a little tighter in the front and said, "Ok. You can talk." Now, I started thinking ahead and was actually looking forward to splitting that money with Denise. Hello! Shopping anyone?

I stared at the screen and he began his story. Although, his screen name was Sterling G, he confessed his first name was Graham. He was a 46 year old divorcee. His wife had cheated on him with her hair stylist then left him. He had been on his own since. He had worked for 6 years in accounting. What was it about bankers and camming? As he continued his story, a couple of other folks in the chat started tipping just to watch me type and talk.

Sterling went on to say that everyone at work thought he was still married because he was too embarrassed to tell anyone that she was gone. He even still wore his ring. Man, I felt really sorry for him. I glanced over at the clock and saw it was already 7:30. That time went by super quickly, especially for 100 tokens and a few other small tips. I looked back at the screen about to sign off, he must have seen my body language because I heard the little slot machine sound go up again.

Then, I heard him say, "I just tipped you 10,000...I think it might be worth a private chat for a minute or two."

10,000 tokens? That's like a thousand dollars. Just to listen? Then I really start thinking. I just made a thousand in less than an hour. What would nine hours be? What was that take home money at the end of the week? And this was just one client?! Oh shit...Then, my analytical mind went into overdrive like a calculator while I processed what to do next.

If the money started rolling in like this, I would never have to save or scrape up money again to pay for any of my patents. I could do it all online. Plus, I could pay my bills in advance if I wanted to and not have to keep dodging those bill collector calls all the time. The most important thing to me was that this was all anonymous. Nobody had to know, except maybe Denise.

Those financial reasons along with the little bit of bravado I was feeling from being admired on cam so openly had me feeling geeked. Alright, let me see what this man is talking about. He did just give me $1,100 just because. Plus, it was only a chat he was asking for. I didn't have to sleep with anybody.

I asked him, "How do I switch to private chat? I've never done it before"

He said, "Click on my profile name and click the button that says private message. Then, click the camera access button. Then only I can see you and I will do the same so only you can see me."

I said, "Done." Since it was just he and I in the chat, I tilted my camera up so he could see my face.

"Girl, you are fine as hell! Oh shit. I didn't know I was talking to a superstar. Thank you for listening to me. I really needed that."

I giggled. Then he continued, "Before you go, could you just pull your robe off your shoulder. It's been so long since I've had a woman's touch or even been close to a woman. I'm too shy to approach anyone but I feel like I can trust you. You seem like a good girl."

"Hold on a second," I told him thinking of the numbers and feeling great. I reached in the mini fridge and grabbed what was left of that little bottle of champagne. Bottoms up. I went back to the screen and thought of what to do next. Just do whatever comes naturally had always been my motto so I did just that. I was still a little hot from browsing those other videos earlier anyway.

I let the robe slip off my shoulder and traced my skin with my finger. Then, I decided to have a little fun. I licked my finger tip and traced the wetness onto my shoulder then slipped my hand into my robe. It was so warm and felt so good to have a hand caress my skin soothingly even if it was my own.

I looked down and realized that my nipples inside the fabric were at full attention again. Wow, who knew this cyber stripper act would turn me on like this. Soooo glad I was still anonymous. I looked up into the screen and I could see his hand going back and forth, stroking himself in the area just below what could be seen on screen.

Wait, was I really doing this? Is he about to come from watching me? But more importantly, is this what it feels like? Somehow this feels a little liberating and empowering.

You see, Victor was never adventurous when it came to doing something a little freaky or new. I had spent so many nights awake in his bed feeling lonely as fuck.

But here, I had 100% of Graham's attention and it felt amazing. I felt so...desired...so in control. And super paid. All of these things combined put me on a high which felt a little different from all of the years I had stayed covered up trying to hide my sexuality.

I stared at the screen watching and listening to his reactions, to me.

"Thank you. You look so beautiful," Graham said as he stroked himself discreetly. "Oh my God, you are amazing..."

I drank his compliment down like a thirsty person in the desert and it fueled me on even more. I took the hand that was inside of my robe and fondled my nipples so they became even more pronounced through the satin of the robe. I slipped the other shoulder out and caressed it with my other hand, all the while to make sure he could only see a little skin, but not too much.

I saw him sit up at full attention and lean closer to the screen. "Oh...yes. You are a goddess!" he said while stroking even faster.

Now I was fully fueled, high on the anonymity of it all and the pure appreciation of this man for my body. I feel like he was caressing me digitally with his eyes and his flattery. Somehow with this rush of hormones, the tips felt secondary but they will still come in handy.

I got totally lost in the moment for a bit as I flicked my nipple gently inside my robe. The wetness from licking my finger soaked through the front of my robe at my nipple and it seemed to be getting him off. Then, I reached over to the other breast and squeezed. "Oh, it feels so good..." I emitted honestly.

He said, "That's right, baby. Let yourself go. You deserve it. That's it. That's it. You are so sweet..." His hand moved even faster.

Oh well, might as well go for it. My body was longing for release and I could feel the heat radiating from between my legs. I continued to play with my nipples while staring at the screen. Yes, it felt good, but I was only going to go so far on camera.

"That's it," he encouraged. "You are so sweet. You are like an angel who came down to talk to me. So perfect. So perfeccct. Ah...ah...ah", he comes. His body jerked a little but I could only see the top half of his body so I didn't get to see the ejaculation. I could just tell from his voice and movements even while he tried to play it cool.

I paused a moment and asked him "Did you just come?"

"Oh yeah," he confessed. "Girl, you are luscious. I could barely help myself. But look, I am not leaving until we make you come. Your body is so hot. Let's make you come, angel. Keep going."

I was ready to get back to the privacy of my bed, but really, so I could come too. Privately. "Maybe we will meet on here again or not," I told him "Have a good night."

"Alright, your body is so fucking fine. Thank you, baby. You made my night. I will be looking for you on here, Princess. Now, I can go and face another day at the office. Thank you so much."

I logged off. I was so affected by this whole scene, which really was not much more than me watching him watching me, but the whole experience of it was making my body vibrate in a way I had never felt before. I headed straight for the bed, without passing go.

I resumed caressing my breasts. Man, this felt amazing. I start stroking between my legs where the heat was radiating. Yep. Soaking wet. It seemed like I could hear his voice talking to me while I stroked it over and over and over, played with my pussy, rubbed the clit, slid my two fingers in and out of the hole and all around my swollen lips until I came.

I...came...so...hard. It was so unexpected, my body shook for what feels like a full 10 seconds. My heart was beating so loudly I could feel it in my ears. I gasped and felt the air as it passed by my lips. I tried to keep control of my body so I wouldn't shake the bed too much and make a lot of noise.

I took my hand still wet with my juices and did something I've never done before. I tasted my fingers for the first time like I had seen a couple of people do on cam. Mmm, it tasted good in a sweet, earthy kind of way, like cake, spices, and peaches.

I laid there quietly for a second and realized that I had just crossed into another realm. Did that all really just happen? I can barely wait to tell Denise what happened online. But also, I needed to ask her how to cash out all of those tips.

Oh, man. Something new altogether was happening with me and I kinda liked it....

CHAPTER 10

The next morning was Sunday. Uncharacteristically, I decided to sleep in instead of going into the office. It was already 9:00. With the prior nights' events monopolized my thoughts, I called Denise to share. I dialed and was totally surprised when she picked up as it was her normal habit to sleep well into the afternoon on Sundays.

"Hal-low?" Denise said dryly, barely awake.

"Good morning. Hey, I just wanted to tell you about last night and ask you a couple of questions. You good?" I said cheerfully.

"Yes, but warning, I haven't had my cup of coffee, yet. Go on."

"Girl…I got on the cam last night."

"Shiiiit! Girl, I'm shocked. Welcome to the club."

"Yeah, yeah. You were right, it is liberating. It was fun. I can hardly believe I did it."

"You lost your camming virginity. Gurrl, you gonna have to tell me all about it. Uh, but first, uh,"she joked, "you can cash out them tips and make sure, uh, I gets my commision."

"Girl! You are crazy!"

81

"Yes. You know you right. Look, I'm gonna go get my coffee and call you right back. I need to be awake so I can get all the details. Chat with you in a sec".

"Girl, bye."

Then,I got out of bed, and was opening my curtains to let the sun in when my phone rang.

Victor's voice was calm on the other end, "Good Morning, beautiful. How was the show?"

I sat down on my bed against my pillows, "What show?"

"The cam show last night."

I was speechless.

He continued, "You were acting a little strange. At first, I didn't know what to think. Then one night I rolled over and you weren't in the bed. I thought you might be in the bathroom but when I got there, it was empty. So, I walked in the living room and there you were, spread eagle on the couch, watching. You had your headphones on so you had no idea I was even there. I watched for awhile then headed back to the room. But you better believe, that next morning, when you were in the shower, I installed a key stroke tracking software on your laptop. I have been watching your moves ever since."

"What...?" I asked him. Still in shock, I hugged one of my pillows and wrapped my blanket around me tightly.

"You could have talked with me about this. I'm not saying I would have approved but at least you could have been honest. Last night, when you went into the private room with that dude, it was the last straw. I am not saying you are a slut. I'm not saying you a whore. I am saying that you are not going to be my future wife."

I started to feel a little panicked, embarrassed, and sad. I planned our future for years. What about our picket fence?

He went on, "I wish you well in everything you do. If you want to be a porno star, the next Kardashian sex tape queen, go for it. Just count me out of that equation. Now, I respect your parents enough that I am not going to embarrass them with this. I trust that can you to handle it. That's all I wanted to say. I love you and care about you a lot but I care about the future I have planned for myself even more. So, I'm out. God Bless, Roxanne."

Barely moving, I croaked, "God Bless you, too, Victor."

He hung up. I laid back down and stared into space. Wow... He knew all these weeks and didn't say a thing. How did I not notice? I thought I had covered my tracks.

All of a sudden, it felt strange not having Victor in my life. I was devastated. I cried into my pillow so no one would hear. Knock knock.

"Who is it?" I asked, wearily.

Candace turned the knob and opened the door. She took one look at my face, stepped inside and closed the door behind her. She said. "What is going on?"

I confessed everything to her...the cams, Victor, everything. Just telling her the story was like opening a fresh wound. It hurt even more. I burst back into tears.

She came over and hugged me like she did when I was five.

"It's gonna be okay," she said. "It was his loss, anyway."

"How?" I asked.

"Look, you are Roxanne Redman, daughter of the Redmans. You are Miss Patents and Royalties who is gonna be a partner at the lab before you're 40. You are an over-achiever in everything that you do. He got mad 'cause some other dude is throwing you some cheese? I'ma keep it real with you. Look, you made that kind of loot and you just started. Some of the women I used to be on the stroll with would kill for that kind of money. And you didn't have to fuck anybody or even touch a dick? Pssst, where do I sign up?"

I stared at her. She continued, "I'm just kidding. What I'm saying though is that you've got a bright future ahead of you, whatever you choose to do."

"Really?" I asked. If anyone was going to judge me, she would.

"Really. Now I gotta go. I was coming in here to ask for five dollars for some gas but now I see you got it like that. So, you got a twenty I can borrow?" she asked.

Used to the routine, I reached in my purse and pulled a fifty out. But instead of begrudgingly handing it her like usual, this time I hugged her and told her, "Thank you. I needed somebody to talk to. Thank you for keeping it real."

"You got it, baby. Gotta go. Thank you and see you when I get back tonight," she said taking the fifty. She patted my head, kissed the bill, and walked out.

I was genuinely grateful for her talk and was feeling better. Inspired even. It felt like I was gearing up for adventure. I was just getting to know these parts of myself. Part of me knew that there was something new and better for me, like a life upgrade.

I was missing Victor, though. He might have enjoyed some of the cam scenes too. We could have watched some together. I thought of all the fun we could have had experimenting with some new positions. But Nana also said, "Coulda, woulda, shoulda means nothing."

So, I had to put Victor in the past now. I took a deep breath of fresh air and held it for a moment before letting it out. It was time to look ahead and sail to whatever shiny, new possibilities the future might hold.

EPILOGUE

Weeks later, Denise and I had dinner with some of our best friends, Hannah and Todd, who were one of the straightest, most traditional couples I knew. They were both interracial. She was Asian and Black and he was Black and White. They both looked like a mix of everything but they got along like two birds of a feather.

For years, these two have seemed happy together which is why I had always had hope for my relationship with Victor. He was ancient history now but he still popped up in my thoughts from time to time. Particularly, when I thought of how glad I was to not be in that situation anymore.

Janelle was also at dinner too. She'd been a friend most of our lives primarily because our parents were friends but we were never really close like me and Denise. I always found Janelle to be really judgmental and a little uptight. But still, she'd always been there for me when I needed her, whether it was someone to shop with when me for a timeless dress for prom or someone who was also driven to study with for finals.

Anyway, halfway through the dinner, right after we placed our dessert order, I let the cat out of the bag. I confessed to the whole table that Victor and I had broken up. Everyone said sorry, including Janelle, but I knew she always liked him. She was probably thinking that now was her chance to go after him. Sneaky bitch.

Then, I revealed what Denise and I had been doing on cam. After my talk with Candace, I felt better about the whole thing and wanted to share it with my friends. Their first response was disbelief.

Hannah almost spit out her water, "You?! Woman, puhleeze. I know you're joking. Ha ha, very funny!" She looked me in the eye and saw that I wasn't laughing.

"You're serious?" she asked.

I nodded and she took a moment, "Wow….ok."

Her husband just listened. She continued, "Well…where do I begin. The first thing I want to say is be safe."

Denise says, "I kind of got her started with it…."

"You? Yeah, why am I not surprised?" Janelle said, with her nose in the air.

"What's that supposed to mean?" Denise asked her.

Hannah jumped in to dispel the tension that was about to pop off, "Believe it or not, I see nothing wrong with it. I mean, we know a lot of people who watch it."

Then, Hannah took a deep breath and said, "I guess I can tell you this now since it was years ago anyways. When I was in college, I danced a little to make extra money so I could come back and forth to visit Todd. He knew about it and even came to one of my shows once. So, I see nothing wrong with it. And by the way, as a long-time married couple, we'd love to hear some of your spicy stories, just for fun of course."

Everyone at the table laughed, except Janelle, who instead said, "Honey, I don't want to know anything about it. You can keep that to yourself. Really, you have so much going on for you. I say, don't do it," she said to me as she sipped her mojito.

I took a closer look at her. Janelle was forever single. I think it was because she found more satisfaction in material things than she would in an actual relationship with a real live person.

Todd sensed the sparks and stepped in and asking, "What I want to know is, what do you like about it? I wondered about that with Hannah too, back then. What do you hope to achieve?"

I paused and thought carefully about my answer, "Well there's the thrill of the game, the rush. Denise would say 'the tips',"

I thought about it a little more and continued, "It's the playing dress up. And another thing that fascinates me are the individual stories of the people. That's what drew me in from the beginning. I mean, who are these people? Why do they do it? How did they get here? How long do they plan to do it? Do their families know? Have they lost anything? Do they gain something? You know?"

Hannah said, "Yeah, I know exactly what you mean. Like the person behind the story. They are acting out a fantasy for the viewer, but like me, some are just acting. They have a life, a past, and probably a real life identity that's actually interesting. Who are these women and men that cam or watch?"

"Exactly," I said. "Sometimes for them it's just about the tips. But other times, the story behind the story is part of the fascination for the people staring at them."

Then, Hannah said five words. I didn't know it at that time but those words were about to change my life, "Why don't you ask them?"

I stared at her and had an aha moment, "Yeah, maybe I will...You know how inquisitive I am. I will ask them!"

Always one to take at a challenge head on, I just let the ideas flow, "I am going to ask them on a show. Like a talk show but a cam talk show. This will have live interviews and I will ask them about their real lives. Plus, they will get to share their kinky stories. My sister Candace always used to say to me, 'You stay perfect.' Ooooh...after all this, what would she say now?"

"While I rarely agree with Candace, we both see eye to eye on that one. Stay perfeccct," said Janelle.

I turned and looked at Janelle, "Are you being serious or sarcastic?"

Stepping over the that potential drama, Denise stayed focused on me and said, "Actually, it's a combination of both of those two words, kinky and perfect, described exactly what you are going through on some deeper level. That sensation of feeling a little kinky but always feeling the need to be perfect. Kinky. Perfect. That has a nice ring to it, Kinky Perfect."

I looked at Denise, "That's going to be the name of our show."

Denise said with a wry smile, "Yes, girl. That describes the show and you to a 'T'. Like a cyber superhero. One way by day, and by night something else completely, honey."

"Thanks, I think," I said dryly, teasing her. Then, I said to Denise, "Hey, you will help me produce it aaand you are going to be my first guest."

"I better go get my hair did then," she laughed.

"I'm serious," I said.

Janelle still sat stone faced. What is wrong with this bitch?

Hannah said, "I like it. Plus, then you can strip or not strip on cam when you want because the show is more about the stories and the people. Yeah, I like this for you." Todd nodded in agreement. They made such a good pair.

Janelle continued to stare in her look-at-me, status drink of the week and swirled it around.

Regardless, I liked this idea. Always a business woman, I immediately started going over some concepts with Denise right there at dinner. We made plans to do the first broadcast next week.

We figured we would broadcast once a week, Fridays at midnight, since I wasn't going to Victor's anymore. We would feature sexy cam stars as guests. They would finally get a chance to share their stories and do a little of their peep show on the air. It was great promotion for everybody.

We could set it up to take tips just like with any other cam room broadcast. The guests would broadcast from their own rooms so they would get to keep all their tips too…. Yeah, this was starting to sound like a plan.

Plus, I know that I got that thousand but how much did the site get? How much were these sites making off the models' cam shows? I asked Denise and she calculated that these sites were getting paid.

"Oh, yeah," I said. "We've got to set it up so we can get some of that, too."

Denise said, "Yes. The entrepreneurial way says have your own… Build it and they will come. No pun intended," she said, laughing at her own joke.

The Kinky Side of Perfect

Denise called a guy she knew named Aaron right there from the table. She said, "He builds websites and knows the inner workings of the web. He would have the tech savvy knowledge to set up this infrastructure properly."

Little did I know that that phone call was about to change my love life forever. She told him the name and concept for the site. Then, she handed me the phone.

"Hello? Hi, this is Roxanne. Denise just explained the basics of the site. What do you think? What else will we need to get it started?"

A man of few words, he replied with a simple, "Love it."

"Cool."

Then he proceeded to give me the technical details of setting it up. He was a little rushed as he explained he was trying to get back to a site migration he was working on. I appreciated the call as was glad to hear everything except for his gruff attitude. But at least hopefully it would be productive working together.

Since the restaurant was fairly empty, I put him on speaker phone sowe could continue to plan. Janelle excused herself, making up some excuse or another. Good riddance

We got back to processing our strategy. We set a preliminary financial goal for this venture at $10 million. Just by coming up with this plan, we knew we were now at least one step closer.

I just hoped that my family didn't find out…or my employers or co-workers. Or Bryce or any other stuck up, uptight people like Ms. Thing here who had just stormed out like a hater.

On the one hand, I would be rich. So fuck them.

Well not my parents, but you get the idea. On the other hand, part of me would still try to cling to my former good girl life as if I could ever go back. Somehow, I knew I couldn't. I had to be blunt with myself.

All of the money, the sex, and that power…I was hooked.

*   *   *

PRESENT

I wake up to the jangle of the suite phone. I look at my watch
and see that I have been asleep for over two hours. Ah, what a
little release can do for a nap. I walk across the room, the
pillow falling from between my legs as I rise.

I answer the phone and am reminded by the caller that I have
signed up for the sunset yoga which starts in 10 minutes. I look
out the window and see the beginnings of a most beautiful
sunset. The breeze is cooler, but not cold. I thank the caller and
hang up. But, I know I won't be going to the yoga class today
because it is almost time for the meetings of all meetings, a
time for my dreams to come true, when I meet my prince face-
to-face. Aaron should already be on the boat, getting settled in
his suite and I need to get ready for our very first rendezvous.

I walk over to the mirror and pat my hair, fish my lipstick out
of my nearby handbag, lean in closer and replenish the red
color of my plump lips. I am just getting to my clothes when
there is a knock at the door. Without bothering to button up my
dress, I move swiftly across the room, swaying my hips gently
in anticipation. I know who it is.

I fling the heavy door open without even looking through the
peephole and throw my arms around Aaron. He is here! His
rock hard penis and granite abs are already calling me through
his jeans and his military green, cotton long sleeve shirt. His
almond eyes, framed by his smooth caramel skin, look wise
like they know every secret of the universe.

It is like our spirits connect without whispering a single word.
We kiss deeply and even though we are face to face for the first
time, it feels sooooo right. This wasn't a fantasy anymore. He
is here. Thank God.

95

The Kinky Side of Perfect

My thoughts wander as to how this came to be. I am so glad that Victor left me so judgmentally. If he hadn't, I never would have discovered true love could be like this.

Aaron slides his tongue in my mouth and I open it wider as I relax and return his kiss. We go deep. It's a relief to be in his arms. His right hand slides to my breast and even though I can see the strength pulsing in his arms, he caresses my nipples with such gentleness, like kissing a flower.

Oh, the chemistry is definitely there. All of those visions of passionate lovemaking on the stairs and in the private elevator in this luxurious gold-accented suite flood back to my mind. I feel so pampered, so safe, and so alive.

This kiss is a magical moment that fills the longing. It feels like the sun, the moon, and the stars are all within our reach. This time, my mind, my body, and spirit are ready. So much has happened already. All of the people I've met, the money I've earned, the lessons I've learned, the stands I've taken. Clearly with the two of us together, this is just the beginning.

I feel like Dorothy clicking her heels at the start of the yellow brick road. Stronger, wiser, healthier, richer and feeling sexier than ever in my life. I silently thank God for this sweet sensation which is the first step on the path to the rest of our lives...which starts now.

THE KINKY SIDE OF PERFECT:

KINKY PERFECT TRILOGY BOOK I

The story continues…

A Kinky Perfect Night: Kinky Perfect Trilogy Book II

Daughters Of Erato: Kinky Perfect Trilogy Book III

If you liked this book, tell your friends.

To receive book updates directly to your inbox,

visit http://kinkyperfect.com/book-updates

for special offers, promos, and more.

STAR SUGARMAN

BIO

Star Sugarman is a writer of top quality erotic literature.

Inspired by the works of the legends such as Zane, Anais Nin, VC Andrews, Karinne "Superhead" Steffans, Bob Gucionne of Penthouse Forum, and E.L. James of 50 Shades Of Grey, she dances to the sexy beat of her own drum like the great luminaries Madonna, Pam Grier, Vanessa Del Rio, and Betty Paige.

D.C. WEST

BIO

An uncertified authority on literary seduction, a martial artist, and studier of tantric arts, DC West's literary influences include Prince, Marvin Gaye, Donnie Hathaway, Leon Issac Kennedy and Rick James. West started reading erotic literature by stealthily sneaking magazines from under his uncle's bed.

Yes, he was looking for the articles but found so much more. He developed a passion for words and images that could express the beauty, joy, and infinite potential of woman. As a child of the 70's and the progeny of Black Power, free love, flower parents, he was encouraged to explore, create, and strive for the best, most engaging, author-reader connection.

KINKYPERFECT.COM

Visit KinkyPerfect.com for your favorite books, fine apparel, sexy accessories, and playful adult costumes.